CAUSE TO SAVE

(AN AVERY BLACK MYSTERY—BOOK 5)

BLAKE PIERCE

D0809596

BOOKS BY BLAKE PIERCE

RILEY PAIGE MYSTERY SERIES

ONCE GONE (Book #1)
ONCE TAKEN (Book #2)
ONCE CRAVED (Book #3)
ONCE LURED (Book #4)
ONCE HUNTED (Book #5)
ONCE PINED (Book #6)
ONCE FORSAKEN (Book #7)
ONCE COLD (Book #8)
ONCE STALKED (Book #9)
ONCE LOST (Book #10)

MACKENZIE WHITE MYSTERY SERIES

BEFORE HE KILLS (Book #1)
BEFORE HE SEES (Book #2)
BEFORE HE COVETS (Book #3)
BEFORE HE TAKES (Book #4)
BEFORE HE NEEDS (Book #5)
BEFORE HE FEELS (Book #6)

AVERY BLACK MYSTERY SERIES

CAUSE TO KILL (Book #1)
CAUSE TO RUN (Book #2)
CAUSE TO HIDE (Book #3)
CAUSE TO FEAR (Book #4)
CAUSE TO SAVE (Book #5)

KERI LOCKE MYSTERY SERIES

A TRACE OF DEATH (Book #1)
A TRACE OF MUDER (Book #2)
A TRACE OF VICE (Book #3)
A TRACE OF CRIME (Book #4)

PROLOGUE

Kirsten braced herself against the Boston cold, adjusted her scarf around her neck, and readied herself for the four-block walk ahead of her, into the black night. She passed all the closed bars, realized it was too late to be walking, and had a pang of sudden fear. She glanced back to the door of the apartment complex she had just stepped out of, and thought of changing her mind. Maybe she should have stayed over at her friend's place.

Amy had insisted that she stay—that it was too late and miserably cold outside. And while both of those things were true, Amy had said them with her face nuzzled into the neck of a guy she'd met at the bar. And while her face had been there, the guy's hands had been elsewhere. And honestly, Kirsten did not want to sleep on Amy's couch while listening to her best friend and some random (but cute) guy going at it in a drunken stupor all night.

Honestly, she also didn't want be there in the morning, working with Amy to come up with a clever reason to get the guy out, either.

Besides, it was only four blocks. And compared to the blistering cold that had ravaged Boston about a month ago, tonight would seem like a brisk little jaunt in a spring breeze.

It was nearing three in the morning. She and Amy had gone out intending to get hammered, to drink the night away and do whatever their drunken primate brains suggested. After all, here, in their senior year of college, their dreams had come true. Somehow, against all odds, they had both been selected out of their photojournalism class—two of eight candidates—to go on assignment in Spain in the summer. They'd be working for an up-and-coming nature magazine that catered specifically to educational markets…and would be getting paid more for that one assignment than Kirsten's mother had made all of last year.

And that would shut her up, Kirsten thought. She loved her mother dearly but got *really* tired of hearing her gripe about how pursuing a career in photography was a pipe dream—a waste of time.

She came to the end of the first block, checked the crosswalk and found it dead, and then headed on. The cold was beginning to nip at her. She could feel it on her nose like an actual presence, starting to pinch.

1

She idly wondered if Amy and her random dude were naked yet. She wondered if the guy was any good or if he'd be hindered by the copious amounts of liquor they'd had.

Well, not that *she* had enjoyed much. She'd eaten a small dinner at the very bar they had holed up in for the night. She wasn't sure if it had been the nachos they'd shared as a table or if it had been something in the pizza, but her stomach had *not* been happy. After four beers, she knew her night was over—that she'd be doing nothing more than keeping Amy company as she annihilated herself shot by shot.

She figured she'd get all the lurid details tomorrow. And thinking of those lurid details as well as how much they'd enjoy their summer in Spain, Kirsten at first barely even noticed the sound she heard behind her. Footsteps.

The hair stood on the back of her neck, but she dared not look back.

She increased her pace. Two blocks behind her, two blocks to go. And now the cold really was nipping at her.

Suddenly, the steps were right behind her, and a man came stumbling up right next to her. He appeared to be drunk and when Kirsten jumped back in fright, he snickered to himself, clearly amused.

"Sorry," he said. "Didn't mean to scare you. I was just…well, can you help me? Drinking with some friends and…supposed to meet them somewhere after the bar but I don't remember where. I'm from New York…never been to Boston before. No idea where I am."

Kirsten couldn't bring herself to look at him as she shook her head. It was more than being uncomfortable around a strange drunk man this late at night. It was knowing that she was *this* close to being home and just wanted the night to be over.

"No, I'm sorry," she said.

"Seriously?!" the man said.

All of a sudden, he didn't seem so drunk. Funny enough, he sounded amused that someone would be so defensive over something as innocent as helping a lost guy in a city he wasn't familiar with. That struck her as odd as she started to turn away, intending to quicken her pace.

But then the slightest motion caught her eye and made her hesitate.

The man was holding his stomach, as if he might puke. It had been there the whole time but Kirsten was fairly certain this was not the case. He reached into his jacket and that's when she saw that he was suddenly holding something.

A gun, her panicked mind thought. And while it *did* look like a gun, that wasn't quite right.

Her muscles demanded that she run. She looked to his face for the first time and saw that something was off. He *had* been pretending. This wasn't a lost drunk man at all. He looked too sober in the eyes—sober and, now that she was starting to panic, a little demented, too.

The thing that looked sort of like a gun came up quickly. She opened her mouth to yell for help as she also turned away to run.

But then she felt something strike her from behind. It hit her in the side of the head, just below the ear—sharp and immediate. She stumbled and then fell. She tasted blood in her mouth and then felt hands on her. There was another of those sharp sensations in her head, small but somehow thunderous at the same time.

The pain was immense but she was not able to experience the full extent of it before the night seemed to swell around her. The street faded, as did the man's face, and then everything went black.

Her final thought was that this life of hers had turned out to be quite short—and that the trip that was set to change it all was never going to happen.

CHAPTER ONE

Avery felt like she had been in some strange isolation chamber for the last two weeks. She had stepped into it of her own accord because, quite frankly, there was no place else that appealed to her—only the sterile walls of the hospital room in which Ramirez still barely clung to the edge of life.

From time to time, her phone would buzz as a call or text came through—but she rarely checked them. Her solitude was only ever broken by nurses, doctors, and Rose. Avery knew that she was probably scaring her daughter. Truth be told, she was starting to scare herself, too. She'd been depressed before—during her teenage years and after her divorce—but this was something new. This went beyond depression and into a realm of wondering if the life she was living was really even hers anymore.

Two weeks ago—thirteen days, to be exact—was when it had happened. It was when Ramirez had taken a turn for the worst after a surgery to repair damage done from a bullet wound that had come less than half an inch from piercing his heart. That turn for the worst had never corrected its course. The doctors said he'd gone into heart failure. He was touch and go; he could come to and fully recuperate at any time or he could slip away just as easily. There was just no way to tell for sure. He'd lost a lot of blood in the shooting—he'd technically died for forty-two seconds following the heart failure—and things just weren't looking good.

All of that had been compacted by the other terrible news she'd received just twenty minutes after speaking to the doctor.

News that Howard Randall had somehow escaped from prison. And now, two weeks later, he had still not been caught. And if she needed a reminder of that terrible fact (which she really didn't), she could see it on the television whenever she deigned to turn it on. She'd sit there like a zombie in Ramirez's room, watching the news. Even when Howard's escape wasn't the headline story, it was still there in the scrolling ticker at the bottom of the screen.

Howard Randall still MIA. Authorities have no answers.

The entire town of Boston was nervous. It was like being on the verge of war with some other nameless country and just waiting for the bombs to start dropping. Finley had tried calling her several times and O'Malley had even poked his head into the room on two occasions. Even Connelly seemed to be concerned about her well-being, expressing it in a simple text that she still looked at in a muted sort of appreciation.

Take your time. Call if you need anything.

They were leaving her to grieve. She knew that and it felt a little silly, seeing as how Ramirez wasn't dead yet. But it was also to allow her to process the trauma of what had happened to her on the last case. She still felt cold thinking about it, recalling the feeling of nearly freezing to death on two separate occasions—inside of an industrial freezer and by falling into frigid waters.

But under all of it was the fact that Howard Randall was on the loose. He had escaped somehow, furthering his already enigmatic image. She'd seen on the news where less than reputable folks on social media were praising Howard for his Houdini-like skills in escaping from prison and leaving no trace behind.

Avery thought about all of this while sitting in one of the recliners that a kind nurse had moved in for her last week, realizing that she was not going anywhere anytime soon. Her thoughts were interrupted by a *ding* from her phone. It was the only sound she was allowing these days, a sign that Rose was reaching out.

Avery checked her phone and saw that her daughter had left a text message. **Just me checking on you,** it read. **You still planted in the hospital? Stop it. Come out and have a drink with your daughter.**

Out of duty more than anything else, Avery responded back. **You aren't 21.**

The reply came right away, reading: **Oh mom, that's cute. There's a lot you don't know about me. And you could learn some of these secrets if you'd come out with me. Just one night. He'll be okay without you there...**

Avery set her phone aside. She knew Rose was right, although she could not help but be haunted by the possibility that Ramirez might decide to finally come to while she was away. And no one would be there to welcome him, to take his hand and let him know what had happened.

She got out of the recliner and walked over to him. She had gotten over the fact that he looked weak, hooked to machines and with a thin tube snaking down his throat. When she remembered why he was here—that he had taken a shot that could easily have been intended for her—then he looked stronger than ever. She ran her hands through his hair and kissed his forehead.

She then took his hand in hers and sat on the edge of the bed. While she would never tell anyone, she had spoken to him several times, hoping he could hear her. She did it now, feeling a little dumb about it at first, like usual, but falling into the habit naturally.

"So here's the thing," she told him. "I haven't left the hospital in nearly three days. I need a shower. I'd like a decent meal and a proper cup of coffee. I'm going to step out for a bit, okay?"

She squeezed his hand, her heart breaking a little when she realized that she was naively waiting for him to squeeze back. She gave him a pleading look, sighed, and then picked up her phone. Before she stepped out of the room, she glanced up at the TV. She grabbed the remote to turn it off and was greeted with a face that she had tried so hard to put out of her mind for the last two weeks.

Howard Randall stared down at her, his mug shot featured on half of the screen while a serious-looking news anchor read something from a teleprompter. Avery clicked the television off in disgust and made her way out of the room quickly, as if Howard's image on the screen had been a ghost, now reaching for her.

***

Knowing that Ramirez had been set to move in with her (and, according to the ring that had been discovered in his pocket after he'd been shot, ask her to marry him) made returning to her apartment a morose experience. When she walked into the place, she looked around absently. The place felt dead. It felt like no one had lived there in ages, a place that was waiting to be stripped, repainted, and rented out to someone else.

She thought about calling Rose. They could hang out and have a pizza. But she knew Rose would want to talk about what was going on and Avery was not ready for that yet. She usually processed things pretty quickly, but this was different. Ramirez being in such jeopardy *and* Howard Randall escaping…it was all too much.

Still…while the place really no longer *felt* like home, she yearned to stretch out on that sofa. And her bed was calling her name.

Of course this is still home, she thought. *Just because Ramirez may not make it and end up here with you, it's still your home. Don't be so damned dramatic.*

And there it was, as plain as day. She'd so far managed to guard her thoughts against that reality but now that it had been dumped into thought form, it was a bit more staggering than she'd assumed.

With slumped shoulders, she made her way into the bathroom. She stripped down, stepped in the tub and drew the curtain, and turned the water to hot. She stood there for several minutes before bothering with soap or shampoo, letting the water loosen her muscles. When she was done cleaning herself, she killed the shower, pushed the stopper down, and ran hot water into the tub. She sat down as it filled, allowing herself to relax.

When the water was at the brim, nearly slopping over the side of the tub, she turned the water off with her toe. She closed her eyes and soaked.

The only sound in the apartment was the slow and rhythmic *drip drip* of excess water from the faucet into the water, and her own breathing.

And shortly after, a third sound: Avery's weeping.

She had kept it in check for the most part, not wanting to show that side of herself in the hospital and not wanting Ramirez to hear it, if he could hear her at all. She'd slipped into the bathroom of his room a few times and cried for a bit but she had never let it come out so freely.

She wept in the tub and, like the thought of Ramirez possibly not making it finally blooming in her head, the crying was also a bit more staggering than she had anticipated.

She let it all out and didn't get out of the tub until the water went tepid and her feet and hands had started to wrinkle. When she finally climbed out, smelling like a normal human again and having soaked in some steam, she felt *much* better.

After she got dressed, she even took the time to put on a little bit of makeup and made her hair look at least somewhat presentable. She then ventured out into the kitchen, poured herself a bowl of cereal as a form of a late lunch, and checked her phone, which she had left on the kitchen counter.

Apparently, she'd been quite popular while she'd been in the bathroom.

She had three voice mails and eight text messages. All of them were from numbers she knew. Two were landlines at the precinct. The others were from Finley and O'Malley. One of the texts was from Connelly. It was the last one that had come in—seven minutes ago—and he was not vague about his purpose. The text read: **Avery, you'd best answer your fucking phone if you value your job!**

She knew it was a bluff, but the fact that Connelly of all people had texted her meant that something was up. Connelly rarely texted. Something big had to be going down.

She didn't bother checking the voice messages. Instead, she called O'Malley. She didn't want to speak to Finley because he pussyfooted around awkward things. And there was no way in hell she wanted to speak to Connelly when he was in a miserable mood.

O'Malley answered on the second ring. "Avery. Jesus…where the hell have you been?"

"In the bathtub."

"Are you at your apartment?"

"I am. Is that some sort of a problem? I saw that Connelly texted. He *texted.* What's wrong down there?"

"Look…we might have something pretty huge down here and if you're up for it, we'd like for you to come in. Actually…even if you're *not* up for it, Connelly wants you here."

"Why?" she asked, intrigued. "What is it?"

"Just…just get down here, will you?"

She sighed, realizing that the thought of returning to work actually appealed to her. Maybe it would give her some energy. Maybe it would get her out of this pitiful funk she'd been in for the last two weeks.

"What's so damned important?" she asked.

"We've got a murder," O'Malley said. "And we're pretty sure it was Howard Randall."

CHAPTER TWO

Avery's dread spiked when she reached the precinct. There were news vans everywhere, complete with scrambling news anchors jockeying for position. There was so much commotion in the parking lot and on the lawn that there were uniformed officers at the front doors, keeping them at bay. Avery drove around back to the other entrance, away from the street, and saw that there were a few vans parked there as well.

Among the few officers at the back of the building keeping the peace, she saw Finley. When he saw her car, he stepped out of the crowd and waved at her, telling her to come to him. Apparently, Connelly had sent him out to serve as a guard of sorts to make sure she was able to make it inside through the throng of craziness.

She parked her car and walked as quickly as she could to the back entrance. Finley drew up next to her at once. Because of her history as an attorney as well as the high-profile cases she'd tackled as a detective, Avery knew she had a face that some local new crews might recognize. Fortunately, thanks to Finley, no one got a good look at her until she was being ushered in through the back door.

"What the hell is going on? We have Randall?" Avery asked.

"I'd love to tell you what happened," Finley said. "But Connelly told me to say nothing at all. He wants to be the first to speak with you."

"Fair enough, I guess."

"How are you, Avery?" Finley asked as they walked quickly to the conference room near the back of the A1 headquarters. "I mean, with everything going on with Ramirez?"

She shrugged it off as best as she could. "I'm okay. Dealing with it."

Finley sensed her cue and dropped it. They walked the rest of the way to the conference room in silence.

She was expecting the conference room to be just as packed as the parking lot. She'd thought something involving Howard Randall would have every available officer in the room. Instead, when she stepped inside with Finley, she saw only Connelly and O'Malley sitting at the conference table. The two men already in the room gave her expressions that were somehow polar opposites of one another; O'Malley's look was one of pure concern while Connelly's expression seemed to say *What the hell am I supposed to do with you now?*

When she took a seat, she almost felt like a kid who had been sent to the principal's office.

"Thanks for coming in so quickly," Connelly said. "I know you've been through hell. And trust me...I only wanted you here because I thought you'd want to be involved in what's going on."

"Howard really killed someone?" she asked. "How do you know? Did you catch him?"

The three men shared an uncomfortable glance around the table. "No, not exactly," Finley said.

"It happened last night," Connelly said.

Avery sighed. She'd actually been expecting to hear something like this on the news or through a text from the A1. Still...the man she had come to know from across a table in prison as she sought his advice and counsel did not seem capable of murder. It was strange...she knew him well from her past as an attorney and *knew* he was capable of murder. He'd done it numerous times; there were eleven murders that were attached to his file when he went to prison and there was speculation that there were many more that could be attributed to him with just a bit more evidence. But still, something about the news shocked her despite it sounding completely normal.

"We're sure it's him?" she asked.

Connelly got instantly uncomfortable. He let out a sigh and stood up from his chair, starting to pace.

"We don't have hard evidence. But it was a college girl and the murder was gruesome enough to make us think it's Randall."

"Is there a file yet?" she asked.

"It's being put together now and—"

"Can I see it?"

Again, Connelly and O'Malley shared an uncertain look. "We don't need you very deep in this," Connelly said. "We called you in because you know this psycho better than anyone. This isn't an invitation to jump into the case. You're dealing with far too much right now."

"I appreciate the sentiment. Are there crime scene photos I can see?"

"There are," O'Malley said. "But they're pretty gruesome."

Avery said nothing. She was already a little pissed that they had called her in with such urgency but were approaching her with kid gloves.

"Finley, could you run to my office and grab the material we have?" Connelly asked.

Finley got up, as obedient as ever. Watching him go, Avery realized that the two weeks she'd spent in a state of uncertain mourning seemed much longer than just two weeks. She loved her job and she had missed the hell out of this place. Just being around the well-oiled machine was boosting her spirits, even if it was only to be something of a resource for O'Malley and Connelly.

"How's Ramirez?" Connelly asked. "The last update I got was two days ago and that update was *still the same.*"

"Still the same," she said with a tired smile. "No bad news, no good news."

She nearly told them about the ring the nurses had found in his pocket—the engagement ring Ramirez had been prepared to offer her. Maybe that would help them understand why she was so close to his injury and had elected to stay by his side the entire time.

Before the conversation could go any further, Finley came back into the room with a file folder that did not contain much. He placed it in front of her, getting a nod of approval from Connelly.

Avery opened up the pictures and looked them over. There were seven in all, and O'Malley had not been exaggerating. The pictures were quite alarming.

There was blood everywhere. The girl had been dragged into an alley and stripped to her underwear. Her right arm looked to have been broken. Her hair was blonde, though most of it was matted with blood. Avery looked for gunshot wounds or stab marks but saw none. It wasn't until she reached the fifth picture that a close-up of the girl's face revealed the method of killing.

"Nails?" she asked.

"Yeah," O'Malley said. "And from what we can tell, they were put in with such precision and force that it had to be one of those pneumatic nail guns. We've got forensics working on it, so we can only speculate the order of it all for now. We *think* the first shot was one that took her just behind the left ear. It must have been shot from a distance because it didn't pierce all the way through. It punctured the skull but that's all we know for now."

"And if that one wasn't the one that killed her," Connelly said, "the one that went in under the jaw, at an angle, sure as hell did. It tore through the bottom of her mouth, slanted in through the roof of her mouth, and tore into her nasal passage and into her brain."

The violence involved does *sound like Howard Randall,* Avery thought. *There's no denying that.*

11

Still, there were other things in the picture that didn't line up with what she knew about Howard Randall. She studied the images, finding that despite all of the cases she had seen, these pictures were among the bloodiest and most disturbing.

"So what, exactly, do you need from me?"

"Like I said…you know this guy pretty well. Based on what you know, I want to know where he might be staying. I think it's safe to say he stayed here in the city based on this murder."

"Isn't it dangerous to just *assume* this is the work of Howard Randall?"

"Two weeks after he escaped prison?" Connelly asked. "No. I'd say it lines up pretty well and *screams* Howard Randall. Do you need to go back and review the photos from the murder scenes from his cases?"

"No," Avery said with a bit of venom. "I'm good."

"So what can you tell us? We've been looking for two weeks now and we're coming up with nothing."

"I thought you said you didn't want me on this yet."

"I need your advice and assistance," Connelly said.

Something about it was almost insulting to her but she didn't see the point in arguing. Besides, it would give her mind something to focus on other than Ramirez's state.

"Every time I spoke with him, he would never just give me a straight answer. It was always a riddle of some sort. He did it to mess with me—to make me *work* for the answer. He also did it just to have some fun on his end. I think, honestly, he viewed me as some sort of acquaintance. Not a friend, really. But someone he could go back and forth with on an intellectual level."

"And he never resented you for all of that drama back when you were an attorney?"

"Why would he resent me?" she asked. "I got him off…a free man. Remember, he essentially turned himself in afterwards. He killed again just to show how incompetent I was."

"But these little visits you've paid him in prison…he welcomed those?"

"Yes. And honestly, I never understood it. I think it was a respect thing. And as stupid as it might sound, I think there's a part of him that always regretted that last kill—of making me look bad in the process."

"And did he ever talk about trying to escape during any of your visits?" O'Malley asked.

"No. If anything, he was comfortable there. No one messed with him. Everyone had this weird sort of respect for him. Fear, maybe. But he was basically king of that place."

"Then why would he break out?" Connelly asked.

Avery knew where he was going with it, what he was trying to get her to say. And the hell of it was that it made sense. *Howard would only break out if he had something to do on the outside. Some unfinished business. Or maybe he was just bored.*

"He's a smart man," Avery said. "Scary smart. Maybe he wanted to be challenged again."

"Or to kill again," Connelly said with disgust, pointing to the pictures.

"Possibly," she conceded. She then looked at the pictures. "When was she found?"

"Three hours ago."

"Her body still there?"

"Yeah, we just came back from the scene. The coroner is due in about fifteen minutes. Forensics is there with the body until they arrive."

"Call them and tell them to wait. Don't touch the body. I want to see the scene."

"I said you're not on this," Connelly said.

"You did. But if you want me to tell you what sort of frame of mind Howard Randall is in—if he *did* commit this murder—then looking at pictures isn't going to do it. And at the risk of sounding cocky, you know I'm the best crime scene investigator you have."

Connelly gave a quick curse under his breath. Without saying anything else, he turned away from her and pulled out his cell phone. He pushed a number through and, a few seconds later, got someone on the other end.

"It's Connelly," he said. "Look. Hold off on moving the body. Avery Black is on her way."

CHAPTER THREE

Oddly enough, Connelly tasked Finley with heading down to the crime scene with her. Finley didn't talk much on the way and instead looked out the window thoughtfully most of the time. She knew Finley had never really gotten deep into the weeds of any high-profile cases. If this was to be his first, she sort of pitied him.

I guess they're preparing for the worst—someone needs to step up if Ramirez doesn't make it through. Finley is just as good as anyone. Better, maybe.

When they arrived at the crime scene, it was clear that the forensics and crime scene investigators were done with their duties. They were milling around, most of them by the crime scene tape looped around the entrance to the alleyway. One of them had coffee in his hand, making Avery realize that it was morning. She checked her watch and saw that it was only 8:45.

God, she thought. *I seriously lost all concept of time over the last few days. I could have sworn it was at least nine when I got to my apartment.*

This thought made her feel tired all in one moment. But she waved it off as she and Finley approached the gathered investigators. She absently waved her badge as Finley nodded politely from her side.

"You sure you're up for this?" Finley asked.

She only nodded as they entered the alleyway, ducking under the crime scene tape. They walked down the alley for several feet and then took a left where the alleyway emptied into small area filled with dust, debris, and graffiti. A few old city garbage bins sat in the corner, neglected. Not too far away from them was the woman Avery had seen in the crime scene photos. Those images had not fully prepared her for seeing it in real life.

The blood, for one, was somehow much worse now. Without the glossy finish of the photos, it was muted and deadly looking. The startling nature of the murder snapped her back to reality quickly, pulling her mind and thoughts almost entirely out of Ramirez's hospital room.

She stepped as closely as she could without stepping in blood and let her mind do its thing.

The bra and underwear aren't sultry or provocative at all, she thought. *This was not a girl heading out in search of a good time. If the underwear looks like this, chances are good her outfit wasn't very revealing, either.*

She slowly circled the body, her mind taking in the small details more than the gore now. She saw the puncture wound where the nail had driven in through the bottom of her jaw. But then she also saw several other wounds, all exactly the same—all inflicted with a nail gun. One between her eyes. One just above her left ear. One in each knee, one in the base of the chest, one through the jaw, and one at the back of the head. The flow of the blood and the brief description Connelly had given her suggested that there were similar wounds on the back of the girl's body, which was currently pressed against the far brick wall like a rag doll.

It was brutal, excessive, and violent.

The icing on the cake was the fact that her left hand was missing. The still-bleeding stump suggested that it had been cut off no more than six hours ago.

She called over her shoulder to the handful of gathered investigators. "Any preliminary signs of rape?"

"Nothing visible," one of them called back. "Won't know for sure until we get her out of here."

She heard the bite to his comment but ignored it. She circled the woman slowly. Finley watched her from a safe distance, looking like he'd rather be anywhere else in the world. She studied the body, the nature of it. This was done by someone who needed to prove a point. That much was clear.

That's why they want to jump straight to Howard, she thought. *He just escaped, was put away for his crimes, and now wants to prove that he's still dangerous—to himself as well as to the police.*

But that didn't feel right. Howard was demented but this was almost barbaric. It was beneath him.

Howard does not have a problem killing—and doing it in ways that grab the media's attention. He scattered the body parts of his victims around Harvard, after all. But nothing like this. This is beyond the point of being obscene. Howard's murders were violent, but there was something almost clean *to them...evidence suggests he strangled them first and then came the cutting. But even the cuts to the severed body parts had been done with something akin to precision.*

When she finally stepped away, logging it all in her head, Finley stepped forward. "What do you think?" he asked.

"I have a thought," she said. "But Connelly sure as hell isn't going to like it."

"What's that?"

"Howard Randall had nothing to do with this."

"Bullshit. What about the hand? Want to bet it's hiding somewhere on Harvard campus?"

Avery only made a *hmmm* noise. He was making a fair assumption, but she still wasn't buying it.

They started back for their car, but before they could even make it to the crime scene tape, she saw a car come screeching to a halt on the sidewalk by the street. She didn't recognize the car but she recognized the face. It was the mayor.

What is this cretin doing here? she wondered. *And why does he look so pissed?*

He stormed toward the remaining investigators, all of whom started to part for him. As they gave way, Avery ducked under the crime scene tape to meet him. She figured she'd cut him off before he could stick his nose in the bloody mess waiting behind her.

Mayor Greenwald's face was a red sheet of pure rage. She was fully expecting foam to start pouring from his mouth.

"Avery Black," he spat, "what in the blue hell do you think you're doing here?"

"Well, sir," she said, not quite certain which smart-assed reply to give.

As it turned out, it didn't matter. Another car came barreling to a stop along the sidewalk, nearly kissing the back of the mayor's. This car Avery *did* recognize. It had barely come to a stop before Connelly got out of the passenger's side. O'Malley killed the engine and stepped out too, catching up with Connelly as quickly as he could.

"Mayor Greenwald," Connelly said. "This isn't what you think."

"This morning, what did you tell me?" Greenwald said. "You told me that all signs pointed to this murder being the work of Howard Randall. You ensured me you would handle the matter with care and that the crime scene might offer clues to where that son of a bitch is hiding. Did you not?"

"Yes sir, I did," Connelly said.

"And you're telling me that sticking Avery Black on the case is *handing the matter*? The very detective that the media *knows* meets in private with him on occasion?"

"Sir, I assure you, she is not on the case. I called her in as nothing more than a consult. She does, after all, know Howard Randall better than anyone else on the force."

"I don't care. If the media smells this…if they so much as *think* Detective Black is running this case, I'll have so much shit to shovel that I'll be using *your* paychecks to buy the shovels."

"Yes, I understand, sir. But the—"

"This city is already terrified with Randall on the loose," the mayor went on, really on a tirade now. "You know as well as I do that at least thirty calls a day are coming in with concerned people thinking they've spotted him. When they get wind of this murder—and let's face it, it's really just a matter of time—they'll know it's him. And if Avery Fucking Black is on the case, or anywhere *near* the case—"

"Then it won't matter," Avery said, having heard enough.

"What did you say?" Mayor Greenwald practically screamed.

"I said it won't matter. Howard Randall didn't do this."

"Avery…" O'Malley said.

Meanwhile, Connelly and Mayor Greenwald looked at her as if she had grown a third arm.

"Are you serious right now?" Greenwald asked.

And before she could answer, Connelly took his side—big surprise there. "Black…you know this is Howard Randall's work. Why in God's name would you think otherwise?"

"Just pull the files, sir," she said. She then looked to Greenwald and added: "Same to you. Check Howard Randall's files. Find one of his murders where he did something like this—something so over the top and bloody. Dismemberment is one thing. But this borders on exploitive. Howard strangled the majority of his victims first. What I'm seeing with this latest death is *far* from something like that."

"Howard Randall smashed one woman's head in with a damned brick," Greenwald said. "I'd say that's pretty bloody and brutal."

"It is. However, that lady was struck twice and the report shows it was the second strike that killed her—not the first. Howard Randall is not in this for the thrill or the violence or the exploitation. Even in scattering the body parts, there was a minimal amount of blood and gore. It was almost as if he shied away from blood, despite his actions. But this murder back here…it's too much. It's gratuitous. And while he's a monster and a definite murderer, Howard Randall is not gratuitous."

She saw a shift in Connelly's expression. He was at least thinking about it, taking her examples with a grain of salt. Mayor Greenwald, on the other hand, was not having it.

"No. This is Howard Randall's work and it's ridiculous to think otherwise. As far as I'm concerned, this murder puts a fire under the entire A1 division—hell, on every officer in this entire city! I want Howard Randall in handcuffs or heads will *roll*. And effective immediately, I want Black off of this case. She is *not* to be involved in any capacity!"

With that, Greenwald stormed back to his car. Avery had suffered through meetings with him in the past and was starting to think he stormed everywhere. She had never seen him simply walk.

"You've been back on the job for half an hour," O'Malley said, "and already managed to piss the mayor off."

"I'm not on the job," she pointed out. "How did he find out I was here anyway?"

"No clue," Connelly said. "We're assuming a news crew saw you leave the precinct and someone tipped him off. We tried to get here before he did but obviously failed." He sighed, collected his breath, and added: "How sure are you that this wasn't Randall? Definite?"

"Of course I'm not *definite*. But this does not fit any of his other murders. This one feels different. Looks different."

"Think it could be a copycat?" Connelly asked.

"It could, I suppose. But why? And if it is, he's doing a bad job."

"What about a fanatical shithead that is into murder culture?" Connelly asked. "One of these losers that collects serial killer training cards got a hard-on when Randall escaped and finally got up the courage to kill for the first time."

"Seems like a stretch."

"So does not fingering a recently escaped Howard Randall for a murder than is so close in style to his former work."

"Sir, you wanted my opinion and I've given it to you."

"Well," Connelly said, "you heard Greenwald. I can't have you helping with this anymore. I appreciate you coming down this morning when I asked but…I guess it was a mistake."

"I guess so," she said, hating how easily Connelly buckled to pressure from the mayor. He'd always done it and it was one of the only reasons she had always found it hard to respect her captain.

"Sorry," O'Malley told her as they headed back to the car. Finley trailed behind them, having watched the entire showdown with passive discomfort. "But maybe he's right. Even if the mayor wasn't being so adamant about this, do you really think it's the sort of thing you should get involved in right now? It's been just over two weeks since your last big case—where you nearly died, I might add. And two weeks since Ramirez…"

"He's right," Connelly said. "Take some more time off. A few more weeks. Can you do that?"

"It is what it is," she said, heading to the car with Finley. "Good luck with this killer. You guys will find him, I'm sure of it."

"Black," Connelly said. "Don't take it personally."

She didn't respond. She got in the car and cranked it, giving Finley only a handful of seconds to join her before she pulled away from the curb and a dead body that she was almost positive was not the work of the recently escaped Howard Randall.

CHAPTER FOUR

Avery was too upset and spiked with adrenaline to go back to the hospital. Instead, after delivering Finley back to the precinct and hopping into her own car, she headed back to her apartment. There were several boxes in the back of her closet that she suddenly felt the need to pull out and look into. More than that, with her mind a little more active and the nip of the real world at her heels, she realized that there was also someone she needed to call.

When she called Rose, her daughter was jubilant at the invitation to come over later for dinner and a glass of wine; they'd ignore the fact that Rose was still sixteen months shy of having a legal drink just for this one night.

When she arrived at her apartment just before 10 a.m., she put on a pot of coffee and threw together two sandwiches. While it was plain old ham, cheese, and mayo on white bread, it was light years above the stale hospital cafeteria food she'd been eating so much of recently. She ate the sandwiches almost absently as she went into her bedroom, opened the closet, and pulled out the boxes that she had pushed far into the back.

There were two boxes, one filled with various files from her brief career as a moderately successful attorney. She was tempted to go fishing through those, as she had actually represented a few people in murder cases. Instead, she went to the box that she knew would provide some insight on what she had seen this morning.

The second box was filled with the files from Howard Randall's case. The case had transpired a little over three years ago but seemed like something she had participated in during some other life. Maybe that's why she had found it so easy and nearly conventional to seek advice and wisdom from him; perhaps she had managed to remove herself far enough away from the case and what it had done to her law career.

The stack of files told a story that she knew inside and out but putting her fingers on the pages and pictures was like sifting through the sands of time, peeking back through the grains to learn some lesson she might have missed earlier. They told the story of Howard Randall, who, as a boy, had been beaten within half an inch of his life by an abusive mother. He was the same boy who would be molested in a high school shower room by a phys ed teacher—a boy who grew to be a man who would not only act out the rage that had built and evolved within him over the years, but also use it to mold and define a brilliant mind that he had never bothered to properly exercise in school. No, he had saved his brilliance for college, starting off in community college to bring up his grades and then impressing the admissions and records offices at Harvard. He'd attended, graduated, and ended up teaching there.

But his brilliance had not stopped there. It had continued on, showing itself in savage ways the first time his hand had grabbed a knife. It had been a knife that had taken his first victim.

Avery came to the crime scene photos of that first victim, a twenty-year-old waitress. A female college student, like all of his victims. There had been one deep gouge in her throat, from ear to ear. Nothing more. She had bled out in the small kitchen of the deli she had been closing up at the time.

A single cut, Avery thought as she looked at the picture. *A surprisingly clean cut. No signs of sexual abuse. In, cut, and out.*

She came to the second image and looked at it. And then the third, and the fourth. In each of them, she drew the same conclusion, ticking them off in her head like a stat sheet to some demented sport.

Second victim. Eighteen-year-old freshman. One cut in the side, seemed accidental. Another one, not so much a cut as a puncture wound with the blade that went directly into her heart.

Third victim. Nineteen-year-old English major, moonlighting as a stripper. Found dead in her car, a single gunshot wound to the back of the head. It was later found out that he had offered her five hundred dollars for oral sex, she invited him back to her car, and he shot her. No signs of her services being rendered were ever found, and in his testimony, Howard confirmed that he killed her before the act was carried out.

Fourth victim. Eighteen years old. Hit in the head with a brick. Twice. First blow seemed to have been too low, did not kill her. Second one crushed her skull and cut into her brain.

Fifth victim. Another slit throat, one deep, steady gash from ear to ear.

Sixth victim. Strangled. No prints.

And on and on. Clean killings. Only copious amounts of blood found at three scenes and that was a matter of circumstance, not theatrics.

So let's say Connelly's hunch and the mayor's belief is right. If Howard is killing again, why change his methods? Not to prove a point—proving a point is macho bullshit that is beyond him. So why would he?

"He wouldn't," she said to the empty bedroom.

And while she was not naïve enough to think that his three years in prison had made Howard Randall a changed man who no longer had an interest in killing, she *did* think he was far too smart to start right up where he left off, in the city that had turned itself upside down to find him in the first place.

If she'd had any doubts before, they were dashed as she looked through the files.

It wasn't him. Still…someone did it. And the assholes I answer to are going to be looking for the wrong man.

***

Avery was both delighted and a little concerned that Rose did not hesitate to drink in front of her. She accepted the glass of white wine with gratitude and thanks, wasting no time taking her first gulp. Avery had apparently been staring in some strange way because when Rose lowered the glass, she grinned and shook her head.

"Not my first glass," she said. "Sorry to ruin any dreams you had of a pristine and saintly little girl."

"Wine will never do that to me," Avery said with a smile. "Some of your past boyfriends, on the other hand…"

"Ooh, nice burn, Mom."

They had just finished a simple dinner of chicken Alfredo and a Greek salad, which they had made together. There was soft music playing in the background, some awful indie pop acoustic drivel that Rose was into these days. Still, the music could not ruin the moment. The city was cast in a cold dark outside, the streetlights gleaming and the gentle rumble of traffic on the street like white noise.

This was exactly what I needed, Avery thought. *Why was I trying to push her away again?*

"So are we just going to dance around the topic of Ramirez all night?" Rose asked.

Avery smirked. It was odd to hear his name come from Rose's mouth…especially just his last name, as if she had known him from work as well.

"No dancing," Avery said. "I just didn't want this night to turn into a sob fest where you had to make sure your mother didn't fall apart."

22

"In a situation like this, it's okay to fall apart a little bit. I just don't know if it's the best thing in the world for you to stay holed up in a hospital room. I mean…isn't it sort of depressing?"

"Sometimes," Avery admitted. "But I'd like to think I'd have someone constantly at my bedside if I was fighting for my life."

"Yeah, I think he'd do the same for you. I mean, I'd be there, too. But at the same time, you know he'd scold you if he knew you were doing it."

"Probably."

"Do you…." Rose started to ask, but then stopped as if she thought better of asking whatever was about to come out of her mouth.

"It's okay," Avery said. "You can ask me anything."

"Do you have a gut feeling about it yet? Like…are your instincts telling you one way or the other that he's going to make it or not?"

It was a hard question to answer. She *didn't* feel strongly one way or the other. And perhaps that was why it was affecting her so badly. There was no certainty. No instinctual nudge that told her he was going to pull through or that he wasn't going to make it.

"No, not yet."

"One more question," Rose said. "Do you love him?"

It was so unexpected that, for a moment, Avery wasn't sure how to respond. It was a question she had asked herself several times in the past—a question that had come to a very distinct and definite answer in the past two weeks.

"Yes, I do."

Rose seemed to beam at this, hiding her smile behind her wine glass.

"Do you think he knows?"

"I think so. But it's not something that we—"

She was interrupted by the sound of shattering glass and a harsh thumping noise. It was so sudden and unexpected that it took Avery roughly two seconds to get to her feet and take in the situation. As she did, Rose let out a little shriek. She had jumped up from the couch and was backing into the kitchen.

The window against the far wall to the left of the couch had been shattered. A cold gust of air buffeted into the apartment. The instrument used to break the window was lying on the floor and made no immediate sense.

There was an old worn brick on the floor, but Avery only spotted that *after* she saw the dead cat. The cat looked to be a thin, malnourished stray. It had been tied to the brick with some sort of rubber strap, like the kind used to tie down canopies or awnings. Broken fragments of glass sparkled beside it.

"Mom?" Rose asked.

"It's okay," Avery said as she ran to the broken window. Her apartment was on the second floor, so while it would have taken some strength, it would have been very possible for someone to make the toss.

She saw no one on the street directly below. She thought about heading out, down the stairs and outside, but whoever threw the brick and cat would have at least a minute's head start on her. And with the busyness of Boston traffic and pedestrians at this time of night (only 9:35, she saw as she checked her watch), he was as good as gone already.

She stepped toward the cat, careful not to step on the glass in her bare feet.

There was a small piece of paper stuffed between the cat's underside and the black rubber tie. She reached down to grab the note, grimacing a bit when she felt the cat's cold, stiff body.

"Mom, what the hell?" Rose asked.

"There's a note."

"Who would do something like this?"

"I don't know," she answered as she plucked the note free and unrolled it. It had been written on half of a torn sheet of basic notebook paper. The note was very simple but still sent a chill through Avery's body.

I'm FREE! And I can't WAIT until I see you again!

Shit, she thought. *Howard. It's got to be.*

It was the first thought in her head and she found herself fighting it off right away. Just like the brutality of the nail-gun murder, something about such a brash statement—sending a dead cat through an apartment window with a threatening note—did not seem like something Howard Randall would do.

"What's it say?" Rose asked, stepping closer. She looked like she was on the verge of tears.

"It's just a dumb threat."

"From *who*?"

Rather than answer Rose, she grabbed her cell phone from the couch and called O'Malley.

From who? Rose had asked.

And as the phone began to ring in Avery's ear, as much as she tried to fight it, there only seemed to be one plausible answer.

Howard Randall.

CHAPTER FIVE

Quite a lot happened in the twelve minutes it took for O'Malley to show up. For starters, the patrol car from the A1 was not the first vehicle to arrive. A news van came to a screeching halt in front of Avery's apartment building. She watched three people get out from her broken window: a reporter, a cameraman, and a tech guy, unspooling cable from the back of the van.

"Shit," Avery said.

The news crew was nearly set and ready to go when O'Malley pulled up. Another car came inching in behind him, nearly careening into the news van. She wasn't at all surprised to see Finley getting out. Connelly was apparently positioning Finley to move up in the ranks—perhaps to even fill Ramirez's shoes.

She scowled at the news van as she watched Finley give the reporter a piece of his mind. There was some brief bickering between them before Finley and O'Malley walked out of sight, toward the stairs that would take them to Avery's apartment.

The moment they knocked on the door, Avery answered it and did not give them a chance to say anything before she let out her concerns and frustrations.

"O'Malley, what the hell? I called you directly rather than the station to *avoid* the news crews. What's their deal, anyway?"

"Their deal is that they're salivating over Howard Randall escaping. And they know you are a familiar face in his history. So they're keeping their eyes on you. I'm guessing this particular crew outside has a scanner."

"Cell phone calls?" Avery asked.

"No. Look, I had to report this to the precinct. It's too high profile. They must have picked it up over radio chatter."

Avery wanted to be furious, but she knew how hard it could be to communicate covertly when a frenzied media was hard at work to break a story. She glared down at the news crew, saw them filming a segment—saying only God knew what. As she watched, another news vehicle pulled up, this one a small-bodied SUV.

O'Malley and Finley looked over the brick, cat, and broken glass. Avery had left the note on the floor, not wanting paper that had been on a cat carcass to sit on her kitchen counter or coffee table.

"I hate to say it," Finley said, "but this looks academic. I mean...*I'm free.* Who else could it be, Avery?"

"I don't know. But...I know you might have a hard time believing this, but it just doesn't seem like something Howard would do."

"The old Howard Randall, maybe," O'Malley said. "But who knows how he changed in prison?"

"Wait," Rose said. "I don't get it. Mom got this guy off when she represented him as his attorney. Why would he come after her? You'd think he'd be thankful."

"You'd think so," O'Malley said. "But that's not how the criminal mind works."

"He's right," Avery said, cutting O'Malley off before he could go on a tirade. "Someone like Howard would see anyone that was involved in the entire process as a threat—even if it was the attorney that managed to get him off. But Howard...this isn't like him. On those few times I went to ask for his help he was...I don't know...*sociable.* If he harbored any ill intent toward me, he hid it exceptionally well."

"Of course he did," O'Malley said. "You think his escape was a fluke accident? I bet you anything this creep had been planning it for months. Maybe even from his first day there. And if he planned on escaping and somehow coming after you or, at the very least, involving you in some deranged plot, why the hell would he let you know it?"

Avery wanted to argue but she could clearly see where he was coming from. He had every reason to think that this note had come from Howard. And she also knew that the city's inherent fear of his escape made it easy for him and Connelly to point the finger in Howard's direction for the nail gun murder.

"Look, let's just put all the Howard Randall stuff aside for the moment," she said. "Whether it was Howard or not, *someone* chucked this thing through my window. I just thought it would be best to go through the appropriate channels since it's clear Connelly wants me as far away from anything that *might* be Howard related as possible."

"I hear that," Finley said. "I got him on the horn on the way here. He's tied up with some business with the mayor and the press right now."

"About Howard Randall?"

Finley nodded.

"Good God," Avery said. "This is getting ridiculous."

"Well, then," O'Malley said, "you're really not going to like what he has ordered me to do."

She waited for O'Malley to tell her. She could tell that he was uncomfortable—that he'd much rather have Connelly here to deliver the order himself. Finally, he sighed and said: "He wants us to relocate you for a few days. Even if Randall didn't throw this brick, it's clear that someone has targeted you and is threatening you. And yes…it's probably because he escaped. I hate to tell you, but you're not looking good in this situation. You got him off all those years ago…sent him off into a killing spree. A lot of people—"

"That's fucking dumb," Rose spat. "People think my mom has something to do with his escape?"

"There are some that have taken it to those extremes, yes," O'Malley admitted. "Fortunately, there have only been murmurs of it on the news. Have you not seen any of it?" he asked, looking at Avery.

She thought of those hazed out moments in Ramirez's hospital room. The TV had been on and she'd seen Howard's face, getting the gist of the reports through the ticker at the bottom of the screen. But she had never seen her name; she'd never expected to. Finally, she shook her head in response to O'Malley's question.

"Well, whatever your feelings on it, I happen to think he's absolutely right. You need to relocate until this dies down. Let's say the person that threw this brick isn't Howard. That means some random citizen threw it. Some disgruntled jerk that thinks you're responsible for a killer being on the loose. So where to?" O'Malley said. "Think it over while you pack a few bags. Finley and I will be happy to take you wherever you need to go."

"No need to think," she said. "I already have a place in mind."

***

They arrived at Ramirez's apartment a half an hour later. It had taken her less than ten minutes to pack the essentials. Rose had also come along, at the insistence of both Avery and O'Malley. After some brief and heated discussion, Rose gave in, stating that she'd stay with her mom for just a day or so…to make sure she was okay.

When the four of them stepped into Ramirez's place, it was a little spooky. While he'd technically agreed to move into Avery's apartment, he'd never gotten the chance. All of his stuff was still there, waiting for him to come home.

Avery moved about the place, pretending it wasn't affecting her. She'd been here several times before and had always felt welcome. That should be no different now.

"You sure about this?" Finley said. "Pardon me for saying so, but it seems sort of sad."

"No sadder than her staying in his hospital room," Rose said.

Avery wanted to let the place soak into her, to get a feel for it and then try to sort out just what she was supposed to do next.

O'Malley was on the phone as they entered, arranging surveillance details for Avery's apartment as well as Ramirez's. They had been very careful about not being followed on the way over, but they certainly didn't want to take any chances.

As Avery set her bag down in Ramirez's living room, O'Malley ended the call he was on. He took a moment, sighed deeply, and looked out the window. Down below, the streets were a little less crowded than they had been when Avery and Rose had been enjoying wine and pleasant conversation. Also, after having a dead cat tossed through her window, it seemed a little more sinister, too.

"So here's the deal," O'Malley said. "For the next three days, you'll have constant look-outs parked out on the street. They'll be in civilian cars, but all members of the A1."

"That's not necessary," Avery said. She was starting to feel like this was all getting out of hand.

"I think it might be," he countered. "You've been in a sort of solitude on this thing for the last few days. It's getting ugly. There are vigilante types out on the street, looking for Randall. People are starting to dig into his history and finding you there."

Go ahead and finish it, she thought. *They're finding me there as the attorney who managed to hand him his freedom—freedom he used to kill one more person. That's what you really want to say.*

But he didn't. Instead, he continued to look out the door. "The first two are going to be Sawyer and Dennison. They'll be here in about half an hour. Until then...looks like it's me and Finley."

Rose looked at the two officers and then at her mother. "Is this...is it really this bad? We need protection?"

"No," Avery said. "It's a bit too much."

"It's for your mom's protection. Yours, too. Depending on who may have been behind the nail gun killing and tossing the brick and cat through the window, you could be in danger, too. It depends on how much of a vendetta this person might have against your mom."

"Let's take the dramatic tone down a notch," Avery said, with venom in her voice. "I'd really rather you not scare my daughter."

"Sorry, Mom," Rose said. "But in the last hour, I've had a dead cat come through your window with a threatening note tied to it and then I was rushed away from your apartment and given round-the-clock police protection. It's safe to say I'm effectively scared."

CHAPTER SIX

Any hope of a quiet girls' night was dashed. When O'Malley and Finley took their leave, the apartment fell quiet. Rose had parked herself on Ramirez's couch. She was scrolling through social media feeds and texting back and forth with her friends.

"I guess you know not to tell anyone what has happened," Avery said.

"I know," Rose said, a bit resentfully. "Wait...what about Dad? Should we tell him?"

Avery thought about it for a moment, weighing the options. If it was just her, there was no question. There was no reason Jack needed to know. But with Rose involved, that changed things. Still...it could be risky.

"No," Avery answered. "Not yet."

Rose only gave a curt little nod in response.

"Rose, I don't know what to tell you. This sucks. Yes. I agree. This is lame. And I'm sorry you're having to deal with it. It's not exactly a picnic for me, either."

"I know," Rose said, setting her phone down and looking her mother in the eye. "I'm not even really upset about the inconvenience. It's not that. Mom...I had no idea things had gotten this dangerous for you. Is it always like this?"

Avery let out a stifled chuckle. "No, not always. It's just that this thing with Howard Randall has everyone looking over their shoulders. An entire city is scared and they need someone to blame while they look for answers and a way to feel safe."

"Shoot straight with me, Mom: are we going to be okay?"

"Yes, I think so."

"Really? Then who threw that brick? Was it Howard Randall?"

"I don't know. Personally, I doubt it."

"But there's some weird...*thing* with you two, right?"

"Rose..."

"No, I want to know. How can you be so sure?"

Avery didn't see any reason to lie to her or to keep her in the dark—especially now that she was apparently a part of this.

"Because a dead cat through a window is too obvious. It's too showy. And despite what the methods of his murders might say, Howard Randall wouldn't do that. A dead cat...it's almost comical.

And in talking to him both as an attorney and a detective…it's not something he'd do. You have to trust me on this, Rose."

Avery looked out the window at the black Ford Focus that sat three floors down, parked along the far edge of the street. She could see the basic shape of Dennison's left shoulder as he sat in the driver's seat. Sawyer would be beside him, probably habitually munching on sunflowers seeds, as he was known to do.

Thinking of the brick and the cat, she started to cycle back through her past. Between her career as an attorney and the few years she'd spent as a detective, the wheel of names and faces in her head was a long one. She tried to think of who else might have reason to toss the brick and cat through her window but it was too much—too many faces, too much history.

Jesus, it could have been anyone…

She turned back to the apartment and tried to envision the last time Ramirez had stood within it. She slowly walked the length of the living room and kitchen, having been there before but seeing everything as new. It was a small place but decorated nicely. Everything was clean and organized, each item in its designated place. His fridge was decorated with several pictures and postcards, mostly from family members Avery had never met but had heard about from time to time.

How many of them know what has happened? she wondered. During his time in the hospital, only two family members had come by to visit. She'd known that Ramirez's family wasn't very close but something about his family not coming to see him struck her as sad—even though she'd likely get the same if something happened to her.

She turned away from the fridge, the images of those strangers suddenly too much for her. In the living room, there were pictures here and there of his life: a shot of him and Finley at a cookout, playing horseshoes; a picture of Ramirez coming across the finish line at a marathon; a picture of him with his sister when they were much younger, fishing along the edge of a pond.

"I can't," she said quietly.

She turned to Rose, hoping she had not heard her audible denial.

What she saw was Rose asleep on the couch. She'd apparently conked out in the moments Avery had taken to look at the photographs. Avery studied her daughter for a moment, feeling the first stirrings of guilt. Rose had no business being here, mixed up in all of this.

Maybe she would have been better off if I'd not reached out to patch things up, she thought.

It wasn't just a wandering woe-is-me thought. She genuinely wondered it sometimes. And now, with both of them under surveillance and people threatening her for sins of her past, it was worse.

Maybe I'm not being threatened for the sins of my past, she thought. *Maybe it was really Howard. Maybe he's snapped in some way I could not have predicted.*

She supposed if she were doing her job correctly, she could not simply eliminate the possibility that Howard had killed that poor girl with a nail gun and then, the next night, tossed a dead cat with a threatening message through her window. She had no evidence to support that he *hadn't* done it so logically, he'd be a suspect.

I'm too close to him, she thought. *I've come to know him in some way that makes me place him on this weird pedestal. Did he intentionally do that?*

It was a scary thought, but he was brilliant. And she knew his penchant for mind games. Had he manipulated her in some way she still did not understand?

She picked up her two bags and carried them into Ramirez's bedroom. She had crammed the basics from the box of Howard Randall case files into one of them before leaving her apartment. She took those out now and fanned them out on the bed.

This time, she did not waste time looking at the photographs. Right now, she just needed the facts. And the facts as she knew them, as had gone down in the books, was that once upon a time, Avery Black had been an attorney who had represented a man who was being accused of murder. She'd suspected that he committed the act but there had been no evidence and the case was getting torn apart in court. In the end, she had won. Howard Randall had been free to go. Over the course of the next three months, college girls from the ages of eighteen to twenty-one were killed in grisly yet effective ways. In the end, Howard Randall had been caught. Not only that, but he openly confessed to the crimes.

Avery had watched it all on television. She had also quit her job as an attorney and had been motivated to start working toward a career as a detective—a career almost everyone told her was out of her reach. She was getting a later start than most. She was a woman who was haunted by the ghost of Howard Randall before his murders. There was too much baggage. She'd never make it.

But here I am, she thought, looking over the details. *Maybe that's why he was always so open to speaking with me in prison.*

Maybe he was among those who thought I was a lost cause in trying to become a detective. When I not only became one, but became a damned good one, maybe I earned his respect.

And sadly enough, she hoped that was the case. She'd like to think that she couldn't care less if Howard Randall respected her— but she did. Maybe it was his intellect or the simple fact that no one had challenged her the way he had when they had occasionally met.

She thought of those meetings while she pored over the case files and it all connected like a frantic tennis match in her head. Back and forth, back and forth.

He genuinely seemed happy whenever I saw him, with the exception of a single time when he thought I was taking advantage of him. He had connections in the prison, able to get knowledge of the outside that other prisoners could not.

Did that information reveal something to him? Did it give him some reason for breaking out other than simple freedom?

And after he broke out, what would he do? What kind of a man would he truly be? Would he get as far away as he could and live life as a free (yet highly wanted) man?

Or would he start killing again? It's been said that once someone commits murder and gets over the initial shock, the second one is easier. And then the third one is almost like a natural act.

But Howard doesn't seem like the type to commit to that base animal instinct.

All of the original murders were clean and simple.

The latest victim was killed in a grotesque fashion...as if the killer was trying to make a point.

Does Howard have a point to prove?

And through it all, she saw him in her mind's eye—sitting across a table from her in the prison with the beginnings of a smile always on his face. Confident. Almost proud.

I have to find him, she thought. *Or at least determine if he is indeed the killer. And the best place to start is going to be speaking to those who knew him on the same level I do. I'm going to have to talk to people he worked with—other instructors at Harvard.*

It felt like a flimsy plan but at least it was something. Sure, Connelly didn't want her on the case, but what he didn't know wouldn't hurt him.

She looked to her phone and saw that it had somehow come to be 12:10 a.m. With a heavy sigh, she gathered the files up into one pile and set them on Ramirez's bedside table. When she undressed for bed, she did so slowly, recalling what things had been like the

33

last time she'd been standing in this bedroom, taking her clothes off.

When she slid into bed, she chose to leave the light on. She did not believe in paranormal activity, but she felt…something. For a brief moment, she thought she could sense Ramirez in the room with her, checking in on her while he floated somewhere between life and death.

And while Avery knew that wasn't possible, she still didn't feel like facing the dark.

So the light stayed on and she managed to fall asleep fairly quickly.

CHAPTER SEVEN

Without any precinct resources, Avery had to rely on the same basic tools as everyone else on the planet. So over a cup of coffee and a few stale bagels she had found in Ramirez's pantry, she pulled up Google and went to work. Because of the case files she'd brought over with her, she already knew the names of three professors who had worked closely with Howard during his time at Harvard. One of them had passed away last year, leaving only two potential sources. She typed their names into Google, clicked her way to the Departments and Staff pages, and saved their numbers into her phone.

As she worked, Rose ambled into the kitchen. She made exaggerated sniffing noises as she headed for the coffeemaker.

"Coffee. Good."

"How'd you sleep?" Avery asked.

"Like crap. And dude…it's seven o' clock and you aren't technically working. So what are you doing awake?"

Avery shrugged. "Not technically working, I guess."

"Won't you get in trouble with your boss?"

"Not if he doesn't find out. Speaking of which…I'm heading out for a bit today. Can I drop you off anywhere?"

"My apartment," Rose said. "If I'm going to be holed up with you for another few days in someone else's place, I'd like a few changes of clothes and a toothbrush."

Avery considered this for a moment. She knew that Sawyer and Dennison were still sitting outside, likely to be replaced by another duo soon. They were likely working in twelve-hour shifts. They'd follow her wherever she went, making sure they remained safe. That could throw a monkey wrench into things. But she already had a plan working out in the back of her head.

"Hey, Rose, where is your car parked?"

"A block over from your apartment."

She'd figured as much. Sawyer and Dennison would automatically ping O'Malley or Connelly if she headed back to her apartment. But maybe if she mixed things up and headed elsewhere, it would be easier.

"Okay," Avery said. "We'll head back to your apartment. I have a call to make really quickly and then I'll see if Sawyer and Dennison can give us a lift to your place."

"Okay," Rose said, obviously skeptical of the plan—as if she knew there was something a little devious about it.

Before she called Sawyer and Dennison, asking for a ride as if she were obeying orders and staying safe, she called a cab company and requested that the driver pick her up at the rear of Rose's apartment building in half an hour.

***

It had been far too easy. And it wasn't that Sawyer and Dennison weren't good cops. They simply had no inclination that Avery would *want* to be disobedient. The way she had it figured, she'd killed two birds with one stone. By slipping out the back of Rose's apartment building unseen, she had a few hours of freedom to do what she wanted without fear of what Connelly would think, while Rose was still under police surveillance. It was a win-win. The fact that she had called to request that they drive them to Rose's apartment had been the icing on the cake.

The cab dropped her off at the Harvard campus shortly after nine o' clock. In the back of the cab, she had called the two professors, Henry Osborne and Diana Carver. Osborne had not answered, but she had managed to speak with Carver, who had set aside some time at ten o'clock to speak with her. With some more hunting around on the Harvard website, she had managed to get Osborne's office location and available times. She figured she'd try hunting him down in the hour or so before she was to meet with Carver.

As she made her way across the campus, occasionally checking the campus map on her phone, she took a few moments to appreciate the architecture. Because most people in the Boston area were so accustomed to the college being in their midst, they often forgot about the history of the place. Avery could see it in most of the buildings, as well in as the overall historic atmosphere of the place—the flawless lawns, the old brick, wood, and landmarks,

She focused on these things as she came to the Philosophical Studies building. Henry Osborne was an instructor in the philosophy school, specializing in Applied Ethics and Philosophy of Language. When she entered the building, a few students were bustling here and there, apparently a little late for their nine o'clock class.

According to Osborne's schedule, he did not have a class until 9:45 and should be available in his office until then. She found his office at the far end of the second hall she came to. The door was cracked and when she peeked in, she saw an older man sitting at a desk, hunched over a stack of papers.

She knocked lightly on the door and took a step inside. "Professor Osborne?"

He looked up with an uncertain smile. When he realized that the woman standing in his doorway was probably not a student, he straightened up and said: "Yes? Can I help you?"

"I tried calling earlier, but there was no answer," Avery explained.

"Yes, I believe I was with a student when my phone rang earlier. Again…what can I do to help you?"

Avery reached into her coat pocket and pulled out her badge. "I'm Detective Avery Black with the Boston police. I was hoping you could lend me a few minutes to talk about your encounters with Howard Randall when he was a professor here."

Osborne gave an exaggerated and breathy sigh, pushing himself away from his desk in frustration. "Absolutely not," he said. "I have nothing more to say about that man. I said all I needed to say when he was at trial."

Avery tried to recall Osborne's face, wondering if he had ever taken the stand during Howard's first trial…when she had gotten him off. She couldn't remember, though something about his face did seem familiar.

"I understand that," she said. "But as you know, he has escaped from prison. And we at the A1 believe that there may be current events that have occurred that mean he might be thinking of becoming active again."

"That's unfortunate," Osborne said. "But I'm not going to offer any more of my time to those horrors."

"But Professor Osborne—"

"I'm not sure there's any other way I can say it," Osborne snapped. "You will not get a single second of my time to speak about him!"

Avery nearly countered with: *Maybe you'll be more willing to talk when more college-aged girls start getting killed.* But she stayed quiet, taking the high road. If he didn't want to talk, that was his right.

"Thank you," she said quietly as she slipped out of his doorway and back into the hall.

She had nearly forgotten just how much of a toll the Howard Randall case had taken on the people around him—co-workers, his thinned out family, and even some of the jurors in the courtroom when he had gleefully admitted to the murders. She supposed the current state of the city's paranoia was further proof of his effect. Clearly, it had imprinted a lasting effect on Henry Osborne.

She took her time crossing campus to reach Diana Carver's office, as she still had thirty-five minutes to spare. She found a coffee shop, grabbed a strong brew, waited outside of Carver's building—the English Department—and called Rose.

"Hey, Mom. You done yet?"

"No. One more quick meeting. I wanted to see if there had been any movement outside with the surveillance."

"Yeah, the guys that had been there were relieved about forty minutes ago. There's some new guys down there now."

"Same car?" Avery asked.

"No. A different car. This one is a Honda. Not sure what style, though."

"Okay. Just…stay put. And if for some reason they need to come up and speak with you, you call me before you answer the door. Okay?"

"Got it. Mom…you aren't out getting yourself into trouble, are you?"

"Of course not," she said.

Though she was thinking: *Not yet.*

***

She found Diana Carver's office with no problems. Avery entered with a bit of reassurance; she had already spoken to Carver on the phone while in the back of the cab and Carver knew why she was coming. She was apparently not totally against speaking about Howard Randall, though she had not seemed particularly excited about it.

Diana Carver was a pleasant-looking woman—the kind who was probably just slightly on the north side of fifty years old but looked closer to a fresh forty. Her shoulder-length black hair looked healthy in the sunlight that came in through her office window, framing her face in a way that made her look both cute and serious at the same time. As Avery took a seat on the other side of her desk, Carver pushed her glasses up onto the bridge of her nose and smiled at her.

"So," Carver said. "This man just won't leave our lives, will he?"

"Excuse me?" Avery said.

"I recalled your name when we spoke on the phone, but wasn't sure why," Carver said. "So I Googled you. You were attorney that first time…when he walked. And then you became a detective that caught a lot of bad press for meeting with him during active cases. So it's clear that Howard never quite left *your* life. As for me…well, I think about him from time to time. He pops up in my head like the memory of some very bad nightmare."

"So I take it you knew him well?" Avery asked.

"Fairly well, yes. At one time I was flirting with the idea of dating him. He never asked me outright, mind you. It was always just something in the air between us."

"Were you ever intimate with him?"

"God, no. The most intimate we ever got was in conversation. Usually over a bottle of scotch in his office."

"And what did you tend to talk about other than work-related things?"

Carver shrugged and for the first time since mentioning Howard, her expression seemed to go a little sour. "A bit of everything," she said. "One of the reasons I was so shocked that he had done those horrible things was because of how brilliant he was. We'd talk back and forth about literature and classical music. It was like something out of a snooty book club or something. I'd lambast Shakespeare and he'd give me hundreds of reasons why he was so popular. He'd tell me why first-person narrative was becoming nothing more than a gimmick for young readers to enjoy while I'd argue its merits. Those were my favorite conversations, but we also discussed current events, social issues, things like that."

"In the course of those conversations, did anything ever strike you as odd? Or maybe even a little extreme?"

"If anything, Howard was quite passionate about *not* liking things. For example, he was very vocal about his distaste for Hemingway. He *hated* Hemingway. He'd get heated over just the mention of the man's name. He'd get angry in those conversations—angrier than you'd expect over a conversation about writers—but not in any sort of threatening way. But when everything came to light, that response in him sort of made sense, I guess."

"Okay, so let's go the other route," Avery said. "As someone who spent some time with him, what would you say were things that really drove him? What made him tick?"

"Being challenged," Carver said right away. "Any sort of challenge, whether it was a friendly argument, competition, or even word search puzzles. That was another thing he'd get angry about—if the crossword puzzle in the day's paper was too easy, he'd get upset. It was sort of silly."

"So these strange bursts of anger over being challenged or things he really disliked...were those the only quirks you ever noticed about him?"

"Well...I mean, I don't know if you'd call it a quirk or not but it *is* one of the reasons I didn't really push to date him. He seemed very uneasy whenever someone would shake his hand. I thought nothing of it at first but then I started to add things up. During one of our deeper conversations, I somehow ended up mentioning that I hadn't had sex in several months. I'm pretty sure I was just sort of letting him know I was available. His comment was something along the lines of 'I haven't had it in longer than that. I never really cared for it.' Or something along those lines."

"So there was no physical contact between the two of you?" Avery asked.

"Oh, I tried to hug him one time...just a way to say goodnight after having a bit too much red wine. When I leaned into him, he went absolutely rigid. For a moment, he looked mortified."

"So your conclusion about him was that he just didn't like physical touch?"

"I suppose. I thought it was just a germaphobe thing when it was just the handshaking. But then learning about his thoughts on sex and his total aversion of something as simple as a friendly hug..."

"There could be some other quirk," Avery finished for her. "Something deeper."

She pondered this for a moment, thinking back over her meetings at the prison with him. Somewhere in the back of her mind, she was pretty sure she'd noticed something similar about him. Whenever she would lean closer across the table when he would whisper something to her, he always either tensed up or seemed to lean back as quickly as possible.

I thought it was just a way to protect his personal space at the time, she thought. *But it also lines up with what Diana Carver is saying—something about an aversion to physical touch. Maybe that played some small part in his bizarre need to dismember his victims...*

She then saw the college girl in the alley in her mind's eye—a girl she didn't even know the name of yet because she wasn't on the case. She'd been stripped down to her underwear, revealing a somewhat thin but well-packaged body.

She then thought of the photographs she'd seen just last night, taken out of her little box of Howard Randall memories.

Yeah, this doesn't line up at all, she thought. *But I should really be sure before I stand firmly behind such a claim.*

"Professor Carver, thank you," Avery said. "You've been an enormous help. And if there is anything you think of in the coming days, please call me directly."

She slid a business card across the desk to her. Carver picked the card up with a frown. "When I heard he'd escaped," she said, "I couldn't help but think how proud he must be of himself. That must have been the ultimate challenge—breaking out of prison. And now he has another one: to escape somewhere without being caught."

"Well, we certainly hope to catch him before he gets too far," Avery said.

"I hope you do," Carver said. "I had never felt like more of a fool in my life. To have considered letting that man into my life—if he'd have had me—and then to find out the kind of monster he really was. It was wretched."

Not knowing what to say to such a thing, Avery again gave her thanks and then excused herself. She instantly called another cab, having sent the previous one away so as to not rack up even more of a fare. After all, these trips were coming out of her own pocket, not the precinct's funds.

With a cab lined up to meet her within ten minutes, Avery sat down on a bench at the agreed upon place and waited. She was pretty sure she knew where she needed to go next if she wanted to solidify her theory that Howard Randall had not killed this latest woman—and that he had probably not been responsible for the dead cat through her window.

Yes, she knew where her next stop would be, but it would be risky. Connelly or, God forbid, the mayor might find out what she was up to.

But it was a chance she had to take. And a chance she felt good about taking as the cab pulled up to the curb. She got into the back seat and gave the cabbie the address to the coroner's office.

CHAPTER EIGHT

One of the many bizarre friendships Avery had made over the course of her career as a detective with the A1 division was with a man named Charlie Tatum. Charlie worked as one of the coroners for the city of Boston, supervised under the city's chief medical examiner. She knew a few other guys in the office, but she'd always had something of a banter-based friendship with Charlie. If she could manage to get alone with him, even if for only five minutes, she was pretty sure she'd get what she needed.

When the cab pulled up in front of the building, she scrolled through the contacts on her phone and called Charlie.

He answered on the third ring with a bored-sounding "Hello?"

"Charlie, it's Avery Black. How are you?"

"Living on the edge, I guess," he said. "We have been instructed not to talk to you."

"By who?"

"The boss man," Charlie said. "As of this morning. I'm pretty sure my boss got a call from your boss and the order was put in."

"Well, I need you to ignore that order. Would you do that for me?"

"I'd have to be sneaky about it," he said. "But yeah. As soon as we were given the order, I was pretty sure that meant I'd end up seeing you before the day was out."

"I'm parked outside in a cab right now," she said. "I need to take a look at a certain file. How possible is that?"

"Hold on one second," Charlie said. She heard him set the phone down and after that, there was silence. The silence went on for about thirty seconds before he came back on. "Maybe we won't have to be all that sneaky after all," he said. "In exactly one minute, just come in through the front doors. I'll take you back to my exam room. You may have to leave out the back when you're done, though."

"That works," she said. "See you in a bit."

This time, she requested that the cab driver hang around so she wouldn't be stuck at a place she was not supposed to be without a ride back to Rose's apartment. As she headed quickly to the front doors of the medical examiner's office, she couldn't help but get a little thrill out of what she was doing. It was one thing to be successfully patching together a potential clue in a new case; it was a whole different feeling to be investigating when she knew she was not supposed to.

Charlie Tatum met her at the front doors, holding one of them open for her. He was a good-looking man, African-American and standing at about six-five. He wasn't exactly fit but still had a sort of domineering presence. She felt it looming over her as she passed by him at the doorway and entered the building.

"Two others are in their exam rooms," Charlie whispered, "and Chambers is working with some of your forensics people on something or another. So you should be good for a while, unless someone finishes up in their exam room."

"Thanks, Charlie. I know you're taking a risk."

"Not a problem," he said as they reached his exam room.

His exam table was empty and the place was clean, yet smelled of chemicals that reminded Avery of death. He locked the door behind them and went directly to the MacBook that was set up in the back corner of the room. It sat on a small counter, with a black rotary stool behind it. Charlie plopped down on the stool and logged into the laptop.

"Fortunately, we have a dummy account for when our own might get locked up," he said. "This way, no one will ever know what I was looking for. So...what *am* I looking for?"

"I don't have a name," Avery said. "But it's a college-aged girl. Twenty-one, I think. Killed yesterday."

"You mean the girl that got killed with the nail gun?"

"Yes."

"That was nasty," Charlie said as he maneuvered the mouse here and there. "One of the worst bodies I'd ever seen."

"But you can access the files from here, right?"

"What we have, yeah," he said. "The body isn't actually here. It's still with forensics. I think they're trying to determine what kind of nail gun would have been used."

"But you've for preliminary information, right?"

"A bit more than that, I think," Charlie said. He gave one final click of his mouse and then got up from his stool. "All yours."

Avery took the stool and scanned over the file. She saw a series of photos of the body and the scene of the crime but those did not interest here right now. She was more interested in the details. She read over them and committed them to memory, not wanting to risk having Charlie print it all out for her.

Kirsten Grierson, age twenty-one. Seven nails placed into her body, two of which could easily have contributed to her eventual death, both having pierced the brain. Light bruising around her lower back which could be a fist. No signs of severe sexual assault, though there were also slight marks and abrasions around the sides of her breasts that indicated the killer had cupped or kneaded them. No fingerprints.

She'd been hoping for more, but still thought she had enough. She looked over the placement of the nails: between her eyes, above her left ear, one in each knee, one in the chest, one through the jaw, and one in the back of the head.

Abrasions on the breasts, Avery thought. *That's not accidental grazing. That's the killer unable to help himself and having a free feel. So it's a man who appreciates a woman's body but is also smart enough to not give in to his lust and add his DNA to the scene. Also...no nails in the breasts or in the vaginal area. If it was a weird sex crime, that would almost be expected as sad as it seemed.*

She thought it all over, then looked at the pictures. The girl was very pretty. And while the bra wasn't anything revealing or particularly sexy, it showed just enough.

The killer appreciated her body. He grabbed her breasts. He also clearly wasn't afraid of blood.

In her head, she juxtaposed that against what she knew of Howard Randall's kills.

No signs of fondling, abuse, or general interest in the women's bodies. They'd all been fully clothed. Excess blood was only found at two sites and it was believed that was because the carotid artery had been severed; the copious amount of blood at those scenes had been incidental, not on purpose.

And that lined up with what Diana Carver had theorized about Howard—that he tried to avoid touching people at all costs.

Doesn't sound like a killer who would risk copping a feel at the last minute, she thought. *Especially not when he had his method down to a science.*

Avery nodded and got up from the stool. "Thanks, Charlie. I'm good here."

"You find what you needed?"

"I did."

"Good. Now get your ass out of here before you get us both in trouble."

***

There was only one other place to go and she knew it was going to result in drama and a lot of yelling. But she felt that she had enough evidence to back up her theory. It was time to head to the A1 and talk to Connelly before this got out of hand—before the city's fixation on Howard Randall allowed a killer to get off without suspicion.

But then there was also Rose to check in on. And Ramirez. She knew it was not her duty but she felt like she needed to drop back by the hospital to check on him. She'd left him nearly thirty hours ago and that was the longest she'd been away from his side since he'd slipped into the coma.

Being by his side won't heal him, she told herself. *And Rose has two cops stationed outside of her apartment. She's safer than you are at the moment.*

She marched quickly for the cab, still waiting for her outside of the chief medical examiner's office. When she got into the back seat again, she wasted no time in giving her destination. There was only one place where she'd actually be contributing anything.

Despite the hellfire that would likely fall because of her presence, she had to go back to the A1.

CHAPTER NINE

She barely made it out of the cab before the gathered news vans recognized her face. She bulldozed her way through them, not giving them a moment of her time. As she made her way to the door, looking straight ahead and doing her best to be unflustered by their swarming, she noticed that they were at least giving her some distance. She wondered how much yelling Connelly had done at them to this point. The thought of it made her smile, but it did not make her any more hopeful about the unscheduled meeting she was about to have with him.

When she finally made it through the doors, she was greeted with a multitude of shocked faces. She also saw some friendly expressions too—those who apparently thought she was being outed simply because of her past. For the most part, though, the feeling in the building seemed to be the same.

You're in deep shit now.

She said nothing to no one as she marched through the front lobby and then into the adjoining hall. She passed a few uniformed officers and then spotted Finley. He was standing in front of Connelly's door, talking to another officer. When he looked up and saw her, he looked worried for a moment. He then seemed to remember that he was technically over her in the chain of command since she had been removed from the current murder case and all things having to do with Howard Randall. He excused himself from the officer he had been talking to and approached her with a scowl on his face.

"What in the hell are you doing here?" he hissed, trying not to draw too much attention. There were already enough eyes on them as it was. Such anger in his voice made him sound like another person altogether. She had never truly seen Finley mad before.

"I need to talk to you and Connelly."

"No. You can't just barge in here and make a scene like this!"

"What scene? Have I been fired? Have I been dismissed? No. So I have just as much of a right to be here as you do. Now—"

Connelly's head suddenly appeared from the around the edge of his door. Her voice had apparently drawn him out. As she had expected, he looked pissed.

46

He narrowed his eyes and practically sneered at her. "Get in here right now," he barked. Apparently, he did not have the same concern as Finley in terms of people hearing a confrontation between them.

She did as asked and traipsed into his office. Helpless to do anything else, Finley followed behind her. He closed the door and stood in the corner, as if waiting for Connelly's wrath to fill the place.

To Avery's surprise, Connelly did a fine job of remaining as calm as possible. He took a series of deep breaths as he sat down in the chair behind his desk. When he was as comfortable as he was going to get, he looked up to her and said: "Why are you here?"

"Because I feel like I have enough evidence to support the fact that Howard Randall did not kill Kirsten Grierson."

"You mean to tell me that while you've been at home, you came up with evidence that we were unable to get with more than twenty men actively on the case?"

"Apparently so," she said.

His patience was wearing thin. He now sat forward with a look of fake chagrin on his face. With a crooked smile, he said: "Please. Do tell me how you cracked this one. And when you're done, why don't you tell me why in the hell you're so determined to separate that maniac from this murder?"

"While we're asking questions," Avery said, "I'd like to know why you've been so insistent on me staying off of this case. Is it because I'm too close to it? Is it because you're afraid how much Ramirez's condition has affected me? Or are you just worried about the bad press?"

"I don't care how close you are to it," Connelly said. "But if I'm being honest, yes…this is the sort of situation the media falls over themselves for. They'll spin some sadistic story out of it. They will tie you to Randall somehow and not only are you going to be tarnished by it, but this whole damned division will be, too! Do you not care about that?"

"Of course I care about that," she yelled. "And if you cared as much as I did, you'd know that taking me off of the case is the dumbest thing you could do. I know your good friend the mayor has deemed it so, but he's not the one in this office all the time, or at the crime scenes, now is he?"

Connelly rubbed at his head and looked down at his desk. "Avery…you have exactly five minutes to tell me what you *think* you have found. You take a second longer than that, and I'll have you escorted out of the building."

"Kirsten Grierson was brutally murdered. There were also marks on her breasts that suggest she was at the very least fondled during the death and staging of the body. She was also in her underwear. The only similar thing about the entire scenario is that she was a pretty twenty-one-year-old college girl."

"Wrong," Connelly said. "You missed the most important detail. And that's the fact that she's dead."

"You know I'm right," Avery said. "You're just blinded by this city's paranoia."

"Don't you tell me—"

"Don't cut in on my five minutes," she barked. "Now...all that blood. The gruesome nature of it. It was too gross. It was over the top. The brutal nature of it was intentional. Now look back at all of Howard Randall's victims and tell me when he acted in such a way. All of his victims were one to two wounds at most. Simple. Clean and precise. It's almost as if he hated blood—as if he really didn't want to touch his victims at all."

"I'm not an idiot," Connelly said. "I've thought of all of this. But it just lines up. Two weeks after his escape, a pretty college girl winds up dead. Maybe he changed in prison. Maybe that confinement broke something in him."

"No," Avery said. "Remember, I met with him a few times."

"Oh, I know all too well," Connelly said.

"He was the same man I defended as an attorney. Whatever weird quirks he had when he was killing...they're still there. He hasn't changed. Not *this* much."

"Okay, so let's say Howard Randall did not kill Kirsten Grierson. Do you have any leads as to who did?"

"No. But it would be simple to run up some sort of a profile. It could be someone who looked up to Howard. Maybe even a copycat who is just a little too bloodthirsty to do it right. Maybe it's someone killing as an ode to Howard—motivated by his escape. Maybe trying to impress him...to get his attention."

"Those are good theories," Connelly said.

From his place in the corner, Finley nodded his agreement.

"But do you know what makes even more sense?" Connelly asked. "Howard Randall—a known murderer of college-aged girls in the Boston area, escapes from prison. Two weeks later, a college-aged girl from the Boston area is murdered. That's a simple equation. All signs point to Randall."

"You're being purposefully closed-minded on this," she said.

"No. *You're* trying to make it into something it's not just because of whatever fucked up connection you have with him."

Avery bit back a stream of curses that wanted to come spewing from her mouth. She clenched her fists, fuming with rage.

"Besides," Connelly said, "you won't have to worry much longer. We've been working on a lead ever since this morning—not that it's any of your business."

"What lead?"

"From an apartment complex. Two different tenants claim to have seen a man who bears a resemblance to Howard Randall sneaking around an old building at the end of their block. That old building just happens to be where one of Randall's victims was found."

"Well then, let's go," she said.

"Too late," Connelly said. He looked at his watch and said, "We've got a team moving in right now. They should be arriving in about three minutes."

Avery's fuming anger turned into shock. She could only stand there in stunned silence as Connelly put on a headset and patched himself through via his phone to one of the officers on site in order to listen as they carried out their orders.

CHAPTER TEN

Eleven miles away from the A1 headquarters where Avery and Connelly were having a tense back-and-forth, O'Malley was quickly stepping out of his patrol car. Three other cars were pulling in behind him, all coming to quick and quiet halts. He waited a beat for everyone to get out of their cars. Including O'Malley, there were five officers in all.

They had all parked on the south side of Commerce Street, adjacent to a rundown apartment complex. Someone from that complex had made the call to the A1, followed by a second less than eight minutes later. Apparently, there was a very good chance that Howard Randall was hiding out in the warehouse that sat along the corner of Commerce Street—the very same warehouse O'Malley was leading the four other officers toward.

It was nearing noon, so the streets weren't as quiet as O'Malley would have liked, but that was okay. This was a derelict part of town—not a part of the city that was going to be clogged with workers rushing to grab a bite to eat on their lunch break. The cracked pavement beneath his feet and the litter strewn against the side of the warehouse was a clear indication of the lack of love and attention these blocks got.

O'Malley looked to the back of his assembled line. This was the line-up he'd asked for—all officers that he knew well and trusted. He knew that Connelly was technically there as well, listening on and present as a live attendant through O'Malley's earpiece.

When O'Malley gave a nod, the officer at the back of the line nodded back and then split off from the group. He drew his sidearm and traced around the edge of the warehouse, taking the back door. The guy's name was Mitcham and it was his duty to catch anyone trying to retreat out of the back...namely Howard Randall.

O'Malley then prepared himself as he marched toward the front door of the warehouse. It was an old metal door that could only be pushed inward. It was covered in tags from graffiti artists. He pointed to the officer beside him and then to the door, making an opening gesture.

The officer grabbed the handle and looked to O'Malley for a signal.

O'Malley drew his sidearm, took a deep breath, and looked at the other three. He gave Mitcham another five seconds to make it around to the back and then nodded.

The officer drew the door open quickly and O'Malley slipped inside with a speed and agility he knew he still possessed but rarely got to display.

The building was one large room, though the fragments of a deteriorated wall were jumbled up along the far side.

In the center of the warehouse, a person was hanging by a rope from a rafter. The rope was tied around their neck and the body hung limply, facing away from them.

A suicide, O'Malley thought. *The crazy bastard killed himself.*

He took another glance around the place, seeing that the other three men with him were doing the same. When it was obvious that they were alone—with the exception of the hanging man that O'Malley hoped to God was indeed Howard Randall—he eased up.

"Chief, you there?" he asked.

He heard Connelly reply in his earpiece, surprisingly crisp. "Yeah. You in?"

"We are," he said, walking to the hanging body. "There's a body. Apparent suicide, hanging by a rope from a steel rafter."

"Is it him?" Connelly asked, clearly excited. "Is it Randall?"

O'Malley approached the body. It was hanging at last ten feet over his head. By the time O'Malley had time to wonder how the man got up to that rafter, he saw the face.

It was smiling.

It had also been drawn on in red magic marker. The "head" was an old burlap sack. The drawn face leered down at him, as if in on the joke.

A small sign was hanging around its neck. It was made of cardboard and the words had been printed in the same red marker that had drawn the face. It read: **FOOLED YA! HEY, HOW'S MY CAT?**

"Fuck!" O'Malley yelled.

"What is it?" Connelly asked.

"He's messing with us," he said. "It's a dummy. He hung a dummy to tease us. There's a note. It references a cat. And it looks like…yeah, it looks like the sign is tied to the dummy with that same black elastic material that was wrapped around the brick and the cat at Black's place."

"It was a set-up," Connelly said.

"Seems that way."

"I want you to go over to that apartment complex and grill the hell out of both of the people that called. If they give you the *slightest* bit of trouble, arrest them and bring them in. I'll deal with making up charges myself if I have to!"

"Yes, sir," O'Malley said.

Frustrated, he holstered his gun and stared back up at the dummy. It was dressed in a back T-shirt and a pair of pants. He was pretty sure that when they cut it down, they'd find it stuffed with straw or old newspapers. It still gazed down lifelessly, giving its red smile.

O'Malley knew it was immature, but he couldn't help himself. He showed the dummy his middle finger as he headed out back to fill in Mitcham.

CHAPTER ELEVEN

Avery had excused herself almost right away after Connelly had ended the call with O'Malley and his team. She'd gone straight for the restroom and locked herself in a stall. She sat on the toilet with the lid down, using it as nothing more than her own private office, wanting to think this through without Connelly badgering her with questions and theories.

The sign on the dummy clearly implies that the man who threw the cat, the brick, and the note through my window is one and the same. And according to the note he tossed through my window, he's interested in coming after me. The note said, "I can't wait to see you again."

But there's no solid link between Kirsten Grierson's killer and the notes or the dummy. It could be two separate individuals and we're just desperate to link them up. It sure would make things easier. And it would make things easier still if the person behind it all just happened to be Howard Randall.

She went over what she knew of Kirsten Grierson's case and the two notes in her head. She looked for a link but there was none to be had—mainly because there wasn't enough information to go on in regards to the identity of the man who placed the dummy and tossed the cat through her window.

Sadly, she was sure that the dummy ruse that had so badly fooled the force was going to be pinned to Howard. And that would give the city all the more reason to demand that he be caught. She supposed she understood the need to blame as much as possible on Howard but if they were wrong on this, they were making a huge mistake that would not be able to be undone.

When she had her head clear, she walked back to Connelly's office. He had managed to swerve his anger of being made a fool of from the person who left the dummy to those who had made the call from the apartment complex. Currently, O'Malley's task force was harassing them, asking why they would have made such a false claim.

When she walked into his office, Connelly looked up at her from behind his desk. There was fury in his eyes but she also saw some fear there as well. She tried putting herself in his shoes, wondering what it might be like to not be able to put his city at ease when a madman was on the loose and a recently escaped serial killer might be behind it all. She pitied him a little.

"So what do you make of the scene at the warehouse?" Connelly asked her.

"I think it was deliberate," she answered. "I don't think the killer was ever there. It was a fool's errand, plain and simple. The killer is laughing at us…having fun."

Connelly scrolled through his phone, pulled something up, and handed it to her. She saw a picture from the warehouse, sent by O'Malley. It was a picture of the hanging dummy from the front. A red smile pointed dumbly down. The sign around its neck could clearly be seen.

FOOLED YA! HEY, HOW'S MY CAT?

Perhaps it was just the way her mind worked—or that she had been working with Connelly long enough now to know what he was looking for.

"It's the same handwriting as the note stuck to the cat," she said. "It's the same guy."

"Howard Randall," Connelly said with stubborn assuredness.

"Not necessarily," Avery said. "With all due respect, sir, I'm growing more and more certain that Howard Randall did not kill Kirsten Grierson."

She saw that he wanted to explode, to chew her out. But he remained calm and, instead, said: "Well, it's a good thing you're not on this case, now isn't it?"

"I guess it is," she snapped back. She nearly gave him a bit of advice, a thought that had dropped into her head when she saw the picture of the dummy and the note. But out of her own interest (and, if she was being honest, just a little bit of spite), she kept it to herself. She'd look into it on her own when she got back home.

"Did you need anything else from me?" she asked, almost under her breath.

"No. We're good for now."

The tension and animosity between them was thick. She could feel it in the room like some weird humidity. Without another word, she turned for the door and left. Outside his office, she took a deep shuddering breath and ran through her options. She looked at her watch and saw that it was 2:25.

I wonder how hard it would be for me to get to that empty warehouse without being seen.

It was a tempting thought but she was pretty sure the trip wouldn't even be worth the risk. That led her to the thought she'd had while standing in Connelly's office.

54

The handwriting on the letter on the cat and the sign on the dummy was a match. Is there any way to get a sample of Howard's handwriting?

For right now, she figured this was the most productive thing she could start working toward. And it would have to start back at Ramirez's place, where she had the materials on Howard Randall's case.

First, though, she needed to get back to Rose—and that meant sneaking back into her apartment building.

But given everything else she had been through in the last six hours or so, that didn't seem like such a difficult task.

***

Knowing that there would be no food in Ramirez's apartment and that Rose herself rarely kept much food in her apartment, Avery stopped by a deli and picked up a few sandwiches for dinner. She caught a cab to the deli but elected to walk the final six blocks to Rose's apartment. Taking a slight detour and coming up behind the building would be much easier than directing a cab to do so. She also figured that anyone who was running surveillance on Rose's place might see the cab and become suspicious. Lord only knew what sort of insane instructions Connelly was giving the officers he tasked with keeping an eye on her.

Not that she resented the choice to keep them under surveillance. A dead cat through a window was bad enough...but when a desperate and anxious media was also involved, she knew things could get dangerous.

It was 3:10 when she came up behind Rose's apartment building from two blocks away. She considered calling to let Rose know she'd be up soon. With everything that was going on, she wanted Rose to be aware of every noise outside of her door. Rose didn't scare easily, but she did tend to make mountains out of molehills. All things considered, Avery thought Rose was handling things exceptionally well.

As she came to the back lot of Rose's building, Avery pulled out her phone, juggling the bag of sandwiches into her other hand. There were only three cars and a city maintenance truck parked in the rear, along with a big blue dumpster for the building and a small pile of cardboard ready for the recycle bin.

No news vans or suspicious cars—which meant no one had figured out this location yet.

Avery scrolled to Rose's number.

Before she pressed it, she caught the shape coming out from behind the blue dumpster. With both hands occupied, she was dearly defenseless.

She dropped the bag of sandwiches but by the time she could get her arm up, it was too late. The shape—which, she now saw clearly, was a man in a hoodie—threw one hand over her mouth while the other caught her free hand and pulled her forward. She tried fighting away and nearly had her arm free, when the man surprised her by sweeping her feet and taking her to the ground.

She managed to keep her head from striking the pavement, but the wind went rushing out of her. Her phone went clattering to the pavement. She heard it, but only distantly. The man had worked fast and continued to do so even now. He locked an arm around her head, her chin caught in the crook of his elbow. He quickly hauled her to a thin space between the building and the back of the blue dumpster.

As she started to collect her wind again, she fumbled for her sidearm but was unable to get to it. The man had her wedged between his right knee and the wall of the building, her back pressed hard to the brick.

His hand pressed hard against her mouth, making it even harder to breathe. Her instincts and training started to kick in. She calmed herself, knowing that fighting hard against her assailant when down and on her back could only make matters worse. Going calm would at least allow her to get a better understanding of the situation.

If he hasn't killed me yet, he doesn't want to. He wants something else. So stop fighting...calm down.

That was easier said than done.

Especially when the man pulled his hood from his head to reveal himself.

She found herself looking eye to eye with Howard Randall.

CHAPTER TWELVE

Panic tried clawing its way back up but she pushed it down—not too hard given the utter shock she felt in that moment.

"That's a good girl, Avery," Howard said.

Their noses were practically touching and when he looked into her eyes there was almost a sort of loving gaze there.

"Sorry I had to be so sneaky," he said. "And rough. But I think you can understand why I had to. Now…before I remove my hand from your mouth and my knee from your chest, I want to ask you two questions. First…are you afraid that I'm going to kill you right now?"

She was surprised to find that she could answer no without any reservation. She shook her head slowly.

"That's right," he said. "And do you think I might rape you?"

Again, she shook her head. The idea of Howard Randall having any sort of sexual interest in anyone was strange to her given what she knew.

"Good," he said. "Now…I'm going to remove my hand from your mouth. If you scream, I won't kill you. I *will,* however, take care of the two cops watching over you. And then I'll kill your daughter. Do you believe me?"

She thought it was a little crude of him to say such a thing. She didn't think he had the physical prowess to take out two cops. But the thought of his hands on her daughter—even his *eyes* on her—unnerved her. So she had no real choice but to nod.

"Good," he said with a smile.

He removed his hand at once. Her jaw eased up as she instantly asked: "What do you want?"

"I want the police off of my back," he said. "You're a smart girl, Avery. I'm sure you've already figured out that I had nothing to do with the murder of that girl. Am I right?"

She nodded. "Yes. But I seem to be the only one."

"So work harder. Convince them."

"Just get out of the city," she said. She realized that he had not yet released his knee from her chest. Apparently, he didn't quite trust her.

Or maybe he does, she thought. *I could call this in. Or, when he lets me go, I could shoot out one of his knees, cuff him, and call Connelly. So why's he here? Maybe...*

But he told her before she could connect the thought.

"I was on my way out," he said. "I truly was. But...well, this new murder is something of a bizarre turn. You're not on the case, right?"

"How did you know?"

"I know because your police friends are terribly predictable. They're trying to pin it on me. And I know there's no way in hell they'd attach you to it. Although, from what I'm seeing, the media is trying to do just that with every ounce of power they have."

"But you—"

"No time for small talk," Howard said. "Listen. I did not kill that girl. And I sure as hell did not throw a dead cat through your window—though that was an inspired move on someone's part. It's too crude for me. And what the killer did to that girl with the nail gun...that was uncalled for. It cheapens the act. It makes it a theatrical gimmick rather than a simple death."

"That's the only reason you're here?" Avery asked. "That's the only reason you risked your neck to have a minute of conversation with me?"

"Of course not," he said. "Since your insipid police force refuses to see this murder for what it is, I figured it's my duty to help...since you *did* always resort to coming to me for help when a case got the better of you. I'm here to help, Detective. I'm here to save you if you need saving."

"You know who did it?" she asked.

Howard only shrugged and smiled. "It could just be a ghost. Someone you can't touch, perhaps. And it looks to be a ghost that would like to haunt me as well."

"Your riddles won't fly right now," Avery said.

"My riddles are all you'll get," he said. "And you damn well better appreciate them."

"Go to hell."

Howard applied a bit more pressure to his knee, crushing her tighter against the brick wall. She bit back a slight cry of pain.

"Now, now," Howard said. "Let's not be an ungrateful bitch. I'm going now, Avery. I'm trusting you. Also, I'm sure you'll understand, but I have to do this..."

Something shifted at her back and then his hand was at her mouth again. But not just his hand. There was a harsh, sharp smell.

Something chemical. Alcohol and something else. On a cloth. She couldn't breathe…couldn't…

Chloroform…

Avery's heart surged with adrenaline and hatred as Howard slowly got up off of her. The moment he did, she tried to scramble to her feet but the chloroform was doing its job. She instantly fell against the side of the dumpster. Her hands tried to raise the gun but, instead, dropped it to the ground.

The last thing she saw before she blacked out against the side of the building was the murky shape of Howard Randall making his way casually across the parking lot.

***

When she opened her eyes, she felt the small headache behind her eyes right away. Slowly, the events of the afternoon came to her in a haze. As she recalled it all, she was more embarrassed than anything. She had been unable to stop him but she still felt as if she had simply let Howard go.

As she got to her feet, her back ached a bit from where he had planted his knee. It almost made her feel as if he was still there. For all she knew, he might be.

Did he jump me just to give me that clue? That riddle?

Or did he jump me because the police pressure is getting to him? Is he scared?

Both of those felt right, and she supposed it was a bit of both. Still, neither option did anything to make her feel any better in that moment. Still collecting her wits, she picked up the bag of sandwiches and her cell phone from the ground. She checked the time and figured she'd been knocked out for roughly twenty minutes, suggesting he'd only given her a slight dose of the chemical.

She waited until she was steady on her feet before she called Rose down to open the back door for her. And even then, she still felt shaken—not quite herself.

Even as she walked inside the building two minutes later with Rose at her side, Avery found herself looking over her shoulder, sure that Howard Randall was spying on her from somewhere close by.

CHAPTER THIRTEEN

They ate an early dinner, Avery not able to swallow much of her sandwich due to the nerves that still seemed to be chaotic over the scare she'd had behind the dumpster. While they ate, she told Rose what had happened, but only because she knew she'd have to tell Connelly. She doubted it would do any good in convincing him and she also knew she would catch hell for letting him go. She figured she could stretch the truth a bit in that area, though.

"Mom, this isn't safe," Rose said after Avery had described the events behind her building. "He knew where you were. He was following you. It's all getting out of hand."

While Rose was overdramatizing things a bit, Avery thought she wasn't too far from the truth. Her attention was being pulled between this new killer—presumably the man who had left the dummy note and tossed the dead cat—and trying to redirect the police away from Howard Randall. And she was having to do it all without the aid of the A1.

And without the help of Ramirez.

Still, she placed the call to Connelly before she could get too derailed. She relayed the same information she had just shared with Rose. Rose listened from her place at the kitchen counter, looking both scared and irritated at the same time. When the call was over, Rose looked at her mother in a way that reminded Avery of a look she'd gotten a lot when Rose had been thirteen or fourteen years old—that stage where her growing teenage girl had criticized everything with a permanent scowl on her face.

"So where are you going now?" she asked.

"You have to come with me, down to the A1," Avery said. "Sawyer and Dennison just now took surveillance duties outside. They're going to take us down to the station."

"I thought they weren't letting you work this case," Rose said.

"They aren't. I think they just feel it safer and more convenient if I'm there."

"So why do I have to go?"

"Because Howard Randall knows where you live. And while I don't think he'd really kill you, I think he *would* go to great lengths to get to me. So you can't be alone right now."

"This is seriously fucked, Mom."

"I know," Avery said. "Now come on. I'm just happy your first time in a police station is as a guest with your mother."

***

At the precinct, she gave a slightly stretched version of what had happened to her behind Rose's apartment. She told it in front of several men, all sitting at the conference room table: Connelly, Finley, O'Malley, Sawyer, and Dennison. Rose also sat at the table, but she was nervously plucking at the corners of her cell phone.

Avery fessed up to having snuck out that morning and then was even honest about what she had done—her trip to Harvard and the coroner's office before her uninvited trip to the A1. Things shifted a bit in the story as she told about getting jumped by Howard. As she told it, she was reaching for her phone as she approached the back door and was assaulted from behind. She claimed that Howard pressed her hard against the wall, which she offered to back up by the bruise on her chest (they didn't need to know it had really come from his knee while he had her pinned behind the dumpster). She then only told them fragments of what had been said. She told them that Howard had professed his innocence to both the recent killing and the brick through the window. He then told her to stay against the wall with her hands behind her head while he retreated or he'd personally kill Rose himself.

When it was all relayed, the men at the table looked around at one another. Avery could practically hear the questions forming in their heads.

It was O'Malley who asked the first one. "Did he say anything about the dummy and the warehouse?"

"Nothing. Which I found off. Maybe he didn't know about it."

"Bullshit," O'Malley said.

"I don't get it," Connelly said. "Why would he take the risk? Why the hell would he assault you?"

"Because that's what he does," O'Malley said. "Because he's violent. Because he's a killer."

"Those are both true," Avery said. "But think about it. He had the chance to kill me. I don't know if he had a gun or not, but he sure as hell got the drop on me. If he'd wanted to hurt me, he had the perfect chance. And then there's the clue he gave me."

"What clue?" Finley said.

"That we might be looking for a ghost—someone I can't touch. And that it's a ghost that might want to haunt him, too."

"And just what in the hell is that supposed to mean?" Connelly asked.

"I don't know yet," she said. "When I met with him at the prison those few times, that's how he always gave me his insights into the cases. It was always with a riddle. Something I had to work for."

"Maybe it's just a riddle to distract us?" Dennison offered.

"Or it could be like the warehouse and the dummy," O'Malley said. "Maybe it's just another way to screw with us and waste our time."

"I don't think so," Avery said. "It's not him."

"You can keep saying that," Connelly said. "But until you come to us with hard evidence of it, we can't—"

"How am I supposed to when you won't let me officially on the case?" she barked, interrupting him.

Connelly was clearly pissed and was looking for an appropriate response when the door to the conference room opened. All eyes in the room turned in that direction and saw Mayor Greenwald enter. He came strolling in as if he owned the place.

I guess he technically does, Avery thought.

Greenwald's eyes first fell on Connelly but when he saw Avery sitting at the table, his face seemed to go three different shades of red. He slammed the door and wasted no time letting the room know how he felt.

"Did I not make myself perfectly fucking clear?" he yelled. His eyes went from Connelly to Avery and then back again. "Avery Black is *not to be anywhere on this case!*"

"And she isn't," Connelly said. He didn't look afraid per se, but Avery could tell that he was choosing his words very carefully. It was odd to see him fall into cover-your-ass mode. "As you were informed yesterday, she has been placed under surveillance. We had to bring her into the station today because, as of about an hour ago, she was attacked behind her daughter's apartment building."

"By who? Was it Randall?"

"Yes," Connelly said.

Damn, Avery thought. *Things would have been a lot easier if he'd have lied about that.*

"And how, exactly, did this miscreant get the best of what I'm told is the best detective in the A1?"

His scowl and rage was turned in Avery's direction now. And as he leered at her, Avery simply could not contain herself. Every ounce of fear and frustration she had felt in the last two days, tied in with the unresolved grief over Ramirez, came pushing to the surface like an erupting volcano.

"That's because you've insisted that you know better than the police," she said. "He got the jump on me because rather than being out there on the streets trying to find your interfering ass some answers, you've chained me like a dog to a post. So I'm a little off my game. A little distracted."

"If you don't watch your tone with me, I'll use your badge as a fucking paperweight," Greenwald said. "Do you understand?"

"A paperweight for what?" she asked. "It seems to me that you're too busy meddling in cases you know jack shit about rather than doing any real work. For starters, why not see what's going on with your prisons? How did someone like Howard Randall escape, anyway?"

Greenwald looked both shocked and surprised. The rage was swept aside, as he was not used to people talking to him in such a way. As he fumbled for words and the rest of the room went quiet with anticipation of a meltdown, Avery felt her phone buzz in her pocket.

She snuck a glance at it, sure it would infuriate Mayor Greenwald even more.

It was the hospital calling.

Ramirez.

She got to her feet and nearly had to nudge past the mayor to reach the door.

"And where in the hell do you think you're going?" the mayor asked.

She ignored him completely, looking over his shoulder toward Connelly and O'Malley. "It's the hospital," she said, swallowing down the fear in her voice.

Connelly nodded and said, "Go. Dennison and Sawyer, can you escort her?"

"And Rose, too," Avery said.

She started for the door, Rose also getting up as Dennison and Sawyer followed. Mayor Greenwald could only watch in confusion, taken off guard by things obviously not going the way he had planned.

On the way out, Avery heard him continue to yell but it was nothing she cared about. She was too busy answering the call from the hospital. Behind her, Greenwald's yelling was no more than distant thunder, groaning and complaining in the distance.

But letting her know, all the same, that there was likely a storm on the way.

CHAPTER FOURTEEN

Avery hadn't even had to ask Rose to stay behind for a moment when they reached the fourth floor. Without a word, Rose detoured toward the waiting room with Dennison and Sawyer and Avery made a near-sprint toward Ramirez's room. As she neared his door, the brief conversation she'd had with the doctor swirled through her head like a breeze.

He's conscious. He's responding to basic stimuli and the only thing he's said is that he wants to see you. I let him know you'd been here for nearly two weeks but got called away. He thought that was funny. I think you should come see him as soon as possible.

That conversation had taken place exactly seventeen minutes ago. Sawyer had driven with the sirens on and ran every red light on the way. And now here she was, angling up to Ramirez's door. When she stepped inside, she had no idea why her eyes started to well up but they did. And she didn't bother wiping the tears away.

He saw her right away. He craned his neck lightly in order to see her but it was clear that it was taking quite a bit of effort. She rushed to the side of the bed and was amazed to see how much more alive he was now, simply because his eyes were open.

"Hey," he said, his voice slightly above a whisper.

"Hey yourself," she said, taking his hand. "Are you okay?"

"Feel a little funny. Groggy. Doc says things look good. A little slow in the thinking department."

"I'm sorry I wasn't here when you woke up," she said. "I was out on—"

"Don't. Doc told me you'd been here almost all day for about thirteen days straight. That was silly. Why?"

Because a nurse found the ring, she thought. But instead, she tried to be funny, although it came out flat. "Nothing better to do, I guess."

Now she finally did allow herself to wipe away some of her tears. They were still coming, though stemming off a bit.

"So what…are you working on now?" he asked.

"I'm not going to talk about that right now," she said, though a part of her badly wanted to. But, of course, not right now. Not after he'd been in something extremely close to a coma for two weeks.

"It'd be more entertaining than what I've been doing for the last two weeks." He chuckled at his own joke and it was clear that it hurt him a bit.

"Can I get you anything?" she asked.

"Some ice, maybe."

"Yeah, I can do th—"

"And a little kiss," he said. "I apologize beforehand about my breath, though."

She gave it to him, gladly. She kissed the corner of his mouth and thought she could feel him trying to return it, but was apparently just too weak.

With the kiss broken, she exited the room and went to the small nurses' station at the other end of the hall. She retrieved a small cup of ice and took it back to his room. In the minute or so it had taken her to get it, though, Ramirez had fallen asleep.

Her heart dropped, fearing that he had fallen back into his comatose state. But as she neared the bed, she could tell that he was in a natural sleep. She wasn't sure how she could tell, but the vague difference in the way his face looked—more natural and relaxed—was enough to set her mind at ease.

She pulled up the chair she had used so much over the last two weeks and simply watched him for a moment. She knew there were things that she needed to tend to very soon but she figured those things could wait for ten minutes or so.

For now, she was going to watch Ramirez. He was alive; he had pulled through.

Everything was suddenly different and she wasn't sure if that was a good or bad thing.

**

After clearing it with Connelly over the phone, Avery had asked that Rose be escorted back to Ramirez's apartment by Sawyer and Dennison. Connelly had agreed, but only if Avery called for an escort whenever she decided to leave the hospital. Rose left willingly enough, but seemed a little misplaced and still unsettled. Avery honestly didn't like the idea of being separated from her but didn't know what else to do. She figured she could talk to Ramirez about it and he'd understand if she left tomorrow morning.

The evening wound into night as doctors and nurses came in and out of the room. With each visit, there seemed to be more good news. The doctors were quick to say that Ramirez would have a relatively lengthy road of recovery ahead of him, but that all signs indicated that he was out of the woods. Early predictions had him leaving the hospital in as soon as a week.

He drifted off twice more, but each time was brief. It wasn't until around ten o'clock or so, when Avery was wired on crappy hospital coffee and the fact that Ramirez was with her again, that he asked her about work again.

"Two weeks stranded in a hospital room with me," he said. "Connelly allowed that?"

Already, his voice was a little stronger, his eyes brighter. "Yeah."

"But like right now, are you on a case?"

"It's complicated."

"Isn't it always?"

"Yes, that's true. But…well, something happened after your injury."

She took a deep breath, realizing that Ramirez had no idea that Howard Randall had escaped. She spent the next fifteen minutes catching him up, telling him about Howard's escape, Kirsten Grierson's murder, the cat through the window, the dummy in the warehouse, and Howard jumping her. She even threw in the part where she had told off Mayor Greenwald in front of Connelly and O'Malley, if for no other reason than to get a smile out of him.

"You sure Randall won't come for you?" Ramirez asked.

"He had his chance," she said. "If he wanted me dead, I'd be dead."

"That's a grim thought," he said, taking her hand and giving it a squeeze.

They sat in silence for a moment and Avery thought he might be on the verge of slipping into sleep again. Instead, he spoke up, saying something that made her think his thought process might not be as sluggish as he had claimed earlier in the day.

"You know," he said. "The whole nail gun thing on this poor girl. It reminds me of something. Some case from way back when."

"Yeah? What case is that?"

"I barely remember it. I was a young annoying street cop at the time. Maybe a year under my belt. Long before you came on and graced us with your presence."

"What do you remember?" she asked. She then thought better of it and added: "But don't think too hard. We still don't know how it'll affect you."

"No, I think it's okay. From what I can remember, there was….some weirdo. Killing women in these really grotesque ways.

66

Choked one with barbed wire. Drove a railroad spike through one's head. Supposedly nailed some mob guy to a barn. He was…"

Avery's blood went cold. "Oh my God," she said, barely in a whisper.

"What?" Ramirez asked.

"I know who you're talking about. Ronald Biel. I represented him when I was an attorney."

"You *what*?"

The words froze in her throat as the details of the case came back.

Ronald Biel, a man who became one of the mob's most feared enforcers—so feared that they eventually cut him loose, and he had not taken it well, going on a killing spree of epic proportions. She'd represented him in court and he had ended up in prison. It had been her fault, working sloppily…on purpose.

"I represented him," she said, starting to feel sick. "It was the only case I ever took on as an attorney that I purposefully lost. I represented him terribly. On purpose. He was guilty. A mob guy that just sort of went off the deep end. He all but *told* me he'd done it, but the evidence against him was flimsy. But he was guilty. I knew it. But the lack of evidence and a contaminated crime scene fucked it all up. He would have gotten off with just a minor sentence. But I wanted him to go to jail…"

"Well, then I guess that's that. If he's in prison, he's not our killer."

"I guess not," she said. "But…in the end, he wasn't charged for the murders. Just collusion and knowledge of the murders."

"How long did he get?" Ramirez asked.

"I don't remember. I'd have to look back through my case files."

"You still have case files from when you were an attorney?"

She nodded, but her mind was elsewhere. She was thinking of Howard Randall's riddle. *A ghost…someone you can't touch.*

"Might be worth looking into," Ramirez said. His voice was soft again, almost dreamlike. A quick look at his face told her that he was falling asleep again—something the doctor told her he might do quite a bit over the next day or so.

Avery positioned her chair, propping a pillow in the right corner of it, and did her best to get comfortable. It was just after eleven when she closed her eyes and attempted to go to sleep.

But there was a ghost haunting her. A ghost from her past.

A ghost…someone you can't touch.

A ghost that might like to haunt me as well…

Howard's voice kept echoing in her head as images of Ronald Biel came to the forefront of her mind.

She recalled Biel well enough. She rarely thought of him, though. After a while all of the demented people she met in her line of work—in both lines of work to this point in her life, in fact—started to blur together. She's lumped Biel in with so many other maniacs she had helped put away as an attorney and detective. The man had one of those faces that seemed like it was *made* for documentaries about the criminally insane. A former mob enforcer with a penchant for gruesome crimes and breaking people's will at any cost. When he had been told that his spree of murders had been all connected, starting at a dingy dock along the Boston Port, Biel had taken to whistling the refrain from "Sitting on the Dock of the Bay."

He'd done it over and over again as a way to taunt Avery as day after day went by and the prosecution failed to come up with any evidence of his crimes. He'd whistle it and give her this creepy smile that seemed to say: *You and I, we're going to win this fucking thing...*

She heard him whistling it even then, remembering it all. It made the hospital room seem all the more enclosed and depressing.

She slept fitfully, waking on occasion and checking on Ramirez. He was sleeping peacefully, even snoring a bit. When she woke up at 5:45, she knew there was no further hope of sleep. Ramirez, meanwhile, was still dozing deeply.

She knew she needed to make a call, but it was too early to do so. She filled her time with grabbing a cup of coffee and walking around the fourth floor to stretch her legs. She checked her phone as she did so. A text message from Sawyer informed her that Rose was fine and that they would be swapping out with another pair of cops for the night shift, to return in the morning around eight or so.

It was driving her crazy to not have access to her files, sitting in a box at Ramirez's apartment. She thought about calling a cab to go retrieve them but thought better of it. She was pretty sure she'd have to sneak around later in the day, away from any of Connelly's surveillance. No sense in pushing things.

She went back to Ramirez's room and found him still sleeping. She turned the TV on, muted it, and watched the morning news scroll by. From what she could tell, the news of Howard Randall was brief—a rehash of news they already knew. She was surprised yet relieved to find that there was no footage from her apartment, the broken window highlighted by some overly dramatic headline.

As she watched it, Ramirez's voice broke her concentration. "Still here?" he asked.

"Yeah."

"Don't do that. Go home. Or to the A1. Or to Rose. I feel like I'm holding you hostage."

"I'm probably going to leave soon," she said. She looked at her watch and saw that she had another five minutes before eight o'clock—when the office she needed to call would open.

"Hot on a trail?" he asked with a sleepy smile.

"Sort of. How are you feeling?"

"Better," he said. "I'd really like to talk to a doctor about trying to go to the bathroom like a normal human being today, though."

She walked over to him and kissed him on the cheek. "I'll see what I can do to get someone to come talk to you when I step out to make a call in a second."

"Hey, Avery? Look...I appreciate you being here with me." His eyes seemed to wander around the room, as if searching for something.

I wonder if he's trying to figure out where the ring is, she thought. *Maybe I should tell him the nurse found it and gave it to me...*

"No problem," she said.

"I love you, Avery," he said. "You know that, right?"

She nodded. "I love you, too."

She kissed him again, on the corner of the mouth. Her heart felt like it was swelling when she pulled away and looked down at him.

A knock on the door broke the moment. She turned and saw Ramirez's primary doctor stepping in. "Sorry," he said, realizing he had just interrupted something.

"No worries," Avery said, stepping back and still a little overcome with emotion. "He was just telling me how much he'd like to pee like a real man today."

The doctor chuckled as he approached the bedside. "Great. I was coming to talk about that very thing."

"On that note," Avery said, nodding toward the door. "I'll be back soon," she said.

Ramirez waved her off, but there was a softness to his eyes she had never seen before.

He just told me he loved me, she said. *And I shot it right back. Something is different now—something great and unexpected.*

She smiled at him and left the room. She grabbed another coffee from the nurses' station and then headed to the waiting room. It was still mostly quiet, only occupied by two people, one of whom

69

was asleep. Avery sat down in the far corner and placed the call she'd been thinking about since last night.

She had to Google the number but found it quickly—the number for the Department of Corrections. After being ping-ponged between a few people, she finally came to the line she was looking for.

"This is Detective Avery White, with the A1 Division," she said. "I'm looking for some information on an inmate's sentence."

"What's the inmate's name?" a robotic-like woman asked from the other end.

"Ronald Biel."

Avery listened to the clicking and clacking from the woman's end, but it did not last long. The woman was back ten seconds later with results.

"Ronald Biel was sentenced to seven years," the woman said. "The sentence was reduced, however, due to exemplary behavior."

"What?" Avery said, flabbergasted. "Shortened by how much?"

"A little less than a year. He was released three weeks ago."

Avery nearly dropped her phone in shock.

A ghost...haunting me...

As if on cue, she heard that damned whistling—Biel, whistling the solo from "Sitting on the Dock of the Bay."

"Thank you," she said dryly into the phone.

Although the shock to her system was deep, Avery instantly got to her feet and headed for the elevators, rushing as if there were a literal ghost on her heels.

CHAPTER FIFTEEN

She decided when she stepped out into the street that she was done with catching cabs. She wasn't sure Connelly would go so far as to have officers on the lookout for her car so she decided to take the risk. She hailed a cab and directed the driver to head to her apartment. As she made her way into the building, she pulled out her phone and placed a call that she did *not* want to make.

But she had to try, at least.

Connelly's phone rang five times before voice mail picked it up. She decided not to leave a message, opting instead to call O'Malley. O'Malley answered on the second ring, probably at his usual station in the A1 headquarters by the coffee and donuts at such an early hour.

"O'Malley, I'm going to tell you something and I really need you to trust me."

"Shit," O'Malley said. "What are you getting into now?"

"Nothing. But I did remember something. A killer I represented as an attorney, a guy named Ronald Biel. I need you to look up his files. Look at those murders. He was never convicted of them, but it was him. I always knew it. I represented him poorly just so he'd go to jail."

"Not very ethical—"

"Just look them up," she said. "O'Malley...I'm pretty certain he's our killer."

"You just said he was in jail."

"He was released on good behavior three weeks ago."

O'Malley sighed. "Fine. I'll look them up. But just so you know...if Mayor Greenwald knows I'm doing anything you ask, he'll hang us both in a very public place."

"Even if it leads us to catching a killer?"

"Probably. But I'll look into it. If I think there's some sort of connection, I'll put it in front of Connelly."

Avery ended the call and did a very quick freshening up process: a quick shower, brushing her teeth, combing her hair. With a fresh change of clothes, she was out of her apartment within fifteen minutes. As she left, pulling the door closed behind her, she looked back at the broken window. It had been covered with a clear sheet of plastic, but the memory of the brick crashing through while Rose had been sitting close to it was fresh.

A dead cat. A brick through the window. Seems very much like something Ronald Biel would have done. So why the hell did I not make the connection?

Some other inner thought answered her own question. *Because you thought he was in jail. And, like everyone else in this city, you apparently had Howard Randall on the brain.*

With one last look at the shattered window, Avery closed the door behind her and headed for her next stop.

***

It felt like ages had passed since the last time she had stepped foot into the law offices of Seymour and Fitch. Now it was *she* who felt like a ghost, stepping out of one world to haunt the hallways of another. When she entered, she saw a new face in the reception area—a young blonde girl, clearly straight out of college.

"Can I help you?" the girl asked.

"Yes. I need to speak with Ms. Seymour. It's very urgent. Tell her Avery Black is here to see her."

The girl looked at her quizzically for a moment, as if the name Avery Black had rung some bells in the back of her head. Avery waited as patiently as she could, sending a quick text to Rose to occupy her time.

How you doing? she sent.

She was starting to feel guilty. Rose had a job and a life of her own. Yet here she was, under police surveillance because of several different branches of her mother's life. Avery knew that Rose was taking this all as well as possible, not freaking out or blaming her for the current awful state of her life.

When it was evident that she was not going to get an instant response from Rose, Avery pocketed her phone. A few seconds later, the young girl appeared from down the hallway to the left. Behind her, Jane Seymour also entered the room. She was clearly older than the last time Avery had seen her but she still had the sort of charm and confidence that seemed to command the attention of an entire room. Her strawberry blonde hair had been cut shoulder-length, at least six inches shorter than she had worn it when Avery worked there. She had also finally caved in and started to use bifocals rather than contacts.

"My goodness," Jane said. "Avery Black, as I live and breathe!"

72

"It's good to see you, Jane," she said.

The two women met in the middle of the room and hugged in the way that people who had once known each other quite well tended to do after a long absence.

"What brings you here?" Jane asked.

"Nothing good, I'm afraid. Could I borrow a few minutes of your time in private?"

"Of course," Jane said, wasting no time in leading the way back to her office.

As they passed through the hallways Avery had once known like the back of her hand, the sense of being a ghost intensified. She felt like an outsider, like she had no business here. It made her want to get the visit over with as quickly as she could without being rude.

She was temporarily taken aback when they stepped into Jane's office. It was huge and looked exactly the same as it had on Avery's last day with the firm. Rather than sit behind her desk, Jane went to the small conference table at the back of the office. Avery joined her there and got right to the point, dashing any hopes of formalities and small talk without being overly pushy.

"I hate to do it," Avery said, "but I *am* in a rush and this could potentially be an urgent matter. Are you okay if I ask you some questions about an old case?"

"Of course. As long as it doesn't breach client confidentiality."

"I don't believe it will. Did you know that Ronald Biel had been released early due to good behavior?"

"I didn't," she said. "How did you find out?"

"A phone call with the Department of Corrections. Look…I'm here to confess, I suppose. That, and to hope you might be able to provide some information."

"Confess?" Jane asked. "Confess what?"

"I threw that case," Avery said. "I knew the evidence was weak and if I really pushed it, he'd get off with just a slap on the wrist. But I knew he was guilty. He all but told me; it was the way he handled himself and reacted when we weren't in the courtroom. He was guilty as hell and I wanted to see him go to jail. So I half-assed it. And now he's out of prison and there's a good chance he's taunting me."

"How's that?" Jane asked.

Avery took the next few minutes to tell Jane about the cat and the dummy—about the girl who had been killed with the nail gun. She was now convinced that the girl probably didn't even have a connection to Biel. He had just used it as a way to taunt her…to let her know that he was free.

It wasn't Howard Randall boasting about how he had escaped at all, she thought as she wrapped up the description for Jane. *It was Biel, letting me know he was out. He's using Howard's recent escape as a cover.*

"Jesus, Avery, that's terrible," Jane said. "But listen to me. As far as your little confession, don't even worry about that. I would have done the same thing. Hell, I *have* done the same thing a few times, just not quite as drastically. So don't waste your time feeling guilty about that."

"Jane...look. If he's after me or even just taunting me, it's behavior that hints at a vengeful mindset. And if he's after me, he might come for you, too. You own the firm, after all, and you were there in the courtroom a lot of the time during his trial."

"Oh, honey...I'm around psychos all day. It's a job hazard. And besides...from the sound of it, if this guy wanted you dead, you'd be dead already."

"Not if he gets a thrill out of teasing me," she said. "Anyway, the other reason I'm here is to see if you happen to have any files related to that case. I need to find something that has Biel's handwriting on it. Something as basic as a signature would do."

"Oh, I'm sure I have something like that somewhere," Jane said. "When do you need it?"

"The sooner the better. Right away would be great."

"Give me an hour. Can you wait, or do I need to email it to you?"

She considered it for a moment and then shook her head. She had to see Rose. She wanted to check in on her, to let her know about Ramirez and to fill her in on this latest breakthrough.

"Email it to me, would you?" she asked. "There's somewhere I need to be."

"I can do that," Jane said. She then gave Avery a sad sort of smile. "Damn, it's nice to see you again, Avery. But please forgive me for saying that you look absolutely exhausted."

"I'm sure I do," she said. "And no offense taken."

She got up to take her leave when her phone buzzed in her pocket. She assumed it was Rose, finally responding to her text as she fished in her pocket for it. Instead, she saw that she was getting a call from O'Malley.

"Hey," she said, answering the call. "You find something in Biel's history that convinced you?"

"No," he said. "I haven't had time. I've been at a murder scene. Looks like it might he Randall again. Or whoever the hell you think is behind it."

74

"Where?"

O'Malley hesitated before answering. "Listen closely to me. I want you here. Connelly does, too—though he won't admit it as openly as I will. Together, he and I can keep this one away from the mayor for at least an hour. Can you make it out here right away?"

"What's the address?" she asked.

He gave it to her and she responded that she knew exactly where it was. "I can be there in twenty minutes."

She ended the call and looked apologetically at Jane. "I've got to go," she said. "But thanks in advance for your help."

"Any time. And Avery...please take care of yourself."

Avery only nodded as she took her leave. A small part of her wanted to slow down as she left the building, to take in the sights and smells of the place that had, in many ways, defined her. This was the place where she had first learned to handle just how driven she was, the place where she had learned volumes about victory and defeat.

But that felt like a lifetime ago. She barely knew that woman at all anymore.

But apparently, Ronald Biel remembered her just fine.

Maybe it's time I reintroduce myself, then, Avery thought as she got into her car and drove off to meet O'Malley.

CHAPTER SIXTEEN

The crime scene was at a private residence in Winchester. When she arrived, she saw that O'Malley hadn't been kidding; they were doing everything they could to keep the murder under wraps. O'Malley's car was parked in the driveway. There were houses on both sides of the residence, as well as across the street. But no one seemed to be looking on, apparently having left for work or holed up inside and totally unaware.

A single police car was parked along the curb. Avery parked behind the police car and hurried up the nicely kept lawn. O'Malley met her at the front door, his face tight and grim.

"How's Ramirez?" he asked.

"He's doing very well," she said. "And the fact that you're leading with small talk makes me think things are bad inside."

"You'd be correct," he said, stepping aside to let her in. "It's pretty grisly."

Avery stepped off of the front stoop and into a modest middle-class home. The front door led into a small foyer where a shoe mat sat in the corner. The living room sat directly in front of her and she could see blood right away, splattered almost artistically on the walls. A TV situated in the center of the room was on, showing a rerun of *M*A*S*H*.

She made her way into the living room, preparing herself for the worst. As she drew closer, she saw more and more blood as new elements of the living room were revealed to her. There was blood on the couch, on the overturned coffee table, and all over the carpet in thick sections, some of which were still wet.

And then there was the body, sprawled in a heap that was barely recognizable as a human form. It sat between the couch and the overturned coffee table.

O'Malley came up behind her, speaking softly, as if in respect and disgust at the same time. As he did, two other officers entered the room from a hallway to the right. They looked like they were both shaken.

"Mitch Brennan," O'Malley said. "Single, thank God. Fifty-six years of age. Worked as a parole officer. And um…shit. You were right, Avery. Partially, anyway."

"Right about what?"

76

"Ronald Biel. Mr. Brennan was his parole officer. I just had it confirmed about two minutes before you arrived."

Sadly, the admission from O'Malley was not as sweet as it should have been. It was tainted by the sight before her.

Just to Mitch Brennan's left, there was a sledgehammer. The head of it was coated in blood and gore. She looked at the body and did her best to make sense of it. There was blood and there were broken bones. There was what had once been a head, but the top of the skull no longer took any definite shape. A few teeth lay in a pool of blood about two feet away from the body. The right shoulder was basically nonexistent, the arm hanging loosely at a sick angle.

She had to look away. She had a strong stomach, but this…this was beyond brutality.

"I know," O'Malley said. "This is barbaric. I'd hate to be the coroner on this one. I don't even know how you'd run an autopsy."

The two officers who had come from the hallway tried avoiding the beaten mess at all costs. "Nothing worth note back there," one of them said. "Everything occurred out here. The back door was forced open, indicating a break-in."

Avery walked around the living room and did her own investigation. She saw the forced entry by way of the back door in the kitchen, just like the other officer had said. The frame was splintered and cracked. She could also see a large dent on the outside of the door, presumably struck by the sledgehammer.

Back in the living room, she tried her best to figure out the chain of events. If the television was on, chances were good that Mitch Brennan had been watching it when Biel broke in. Maybe he'd made a dash for the front door. Maybe he tried to make it to a gun that was hidden somewhere in the house. Avery couldn't tell. There was just too much blood to be certain of anything.

As she looked around for answers, the sound of the front door opening distracted her. *Mayor Greenwald, no doubt,* she thought. *This could get interesting…*

But it was not Greenwald. Instead, Connelly stepped into the living room. The look of horror on his face was unmistakable and he did little to hide it. He let out an audible gasp as he turned away from it.

"Sir," O'Malley said. "Did you get my message?"

"About this being Ronald Biel's parole officer? Yeah." He then looked to Avery. "I still say that first one was Howard Randall. A young college girl. That was his thing. But this…yeah, even

Randall doesn't have this in him. And the connection can't be ignored."

"There's also the note on the dummy and the one that came with the dead cat," she said. "The first one talked about being free. Now that we know that Biel was recently released, that could have easily been him taunting me."

"Because you stuck his ass in prison?" Connelly asked.

"Presumably." She still couldn't find it in her to admit to throwing his case. It had been hard enough to tell Jane Seymour. It was harder still to tell these two men—men that she worked with closely, men that she knew would protect her while in the field.

"Or maybe it's both of them," Connelly said. "Maybe we have two psychos running around the city."

"What else do you have?" O'Malley asked her. "I know there's no way you've just been sitting."

"I know that Howard Randall was not a fan of physical touch. And Biel seems to revel in goriness. I've also reached out to my former law firm. They're looking for any documents that might have Biel's handwriting. If it's the same as the handwriting on the letter and the sign on the dummy, I think there's no question: it's all Biel."

"Given that and then the fact that we could have two murderers on your bad side, how long would you need to wrap this up?" Connelly asked.

"Sir…" O'Malley said. "The mayor—"

"To hell with Greenwald for now. I'd like to see him come look at this mess," he said, nodding toward the bloodied shape that had once been Mitch Brennan.

"I don't know, sir," she said.

"You're on the case," he said. "Make it quick and work like a phantom. Don't make any scenes. I'll keep Greenwald off of you for as long as I can. And if you can wrap it up before he finds out you're active on it, all the better."

"Yes, sir."

"Also…I'm not going to stick a partner with you. But I am going to inform Sawyer and Dennison to loosen the reins a bit. Anything big comes up, I want to know about it before you act."

"Understood."

"And Avery? I'm glad to hear Ramirez is doing better. When you see him again, give him my best."

Avery took her leave, quickly heading back to her car. With permission to actively work the case, a whole new world of possibilities opened up to her.

The only question now was where she should start.

Biel's grinning, leering face popped up in her head. She heard his gleeful whistling like a dusty wind tearing through her mind.

I had totally put Biel out of my mind these last six years. Maybe I should start by talking to those who last spoke with him.

The prison.

CHAPTER SEVENTEEN

It felt odd to be entering South Bay House of Corrections, knowing that she was not entering in order to meet with Howard. It made her feel like she was visiting as some weird stalker who could not get over her lure of the place. But once she was inside, the feeling was replaced by an urgent sense of duty—the need to get in and out as quickly as possible.

Because of the short notice she had given, Avery was not able to see anyone right away. She knew there were protocols to be followed and forms to be filled out. She understood the need for these regulations, but as she waited in a small holding area, it was frustrating. While she waited, she leafed through a case file of Biel's history that a helpful woman from records had provide her with.

It was uncanny how quickly that time in her life seemed to unfold in her mind's eye as she read through the files and studied the images. Visiting with Jane had also stirred up memories from that time in her life, but the file in front of her was like a jarring slap to the face. She read over Biel's bio as a photograph of his hardened and emotionless face stared out at her.

Ronald Biel had a record that started at the age of sixteen, with a grand theft auto charge in New Jersey. By the time he turned twenty, he'd also been charged with two counts of breaking and entering and had been fingered in a manslaughter case but had gotten off. Four years later, his name started coming up in mob-oriented cases, always a name and face that seemed to be hovering around the scene of crimes or reports. Rumors had started to circulate that Biel was indeed part of the mob scene around New Jersey and an extended arm that had reached further south, as far down as Baltimore, Maryland.

He worked as an enforcer, which, depending on which mob circuit you asked, involved roughing people up for information or to coerce them into doing certain things. Before Biel's already tainted history got even worse, he had copped to busting knee caps, breaking fingers, and plucking out teeth with pliers. But somewhere along the line, something in Biel shifted and he started to get even rougher. Rumors has started swirling around the mob crowd that he was something of a loose cannon, using grotesque methods for his line of work that had some questioning whether or not he might end up drawing unnecessary attention to mob activities. After a few more cases, one of which was rumored to have resulted in the death of the son of a drug lord, the mob disowned him.

However, Biel had made close friends. When he left, they left with him. The mob dropped anonymous tips here and there, hoping to them arrested. This led to a shootout that resulted in the deaths of two FBI agents, one policeman, and three civilians. Biel managed to escape with a few of his associates. They were on the run for three weeks and the active manhunt might have lasted longer had Biel not apparently snapped.

The hunt came to a stall when one of Biel's runaway associates was found dead on an overpass along the Beltway. His throat had been cut and he had been partially disemboweled. The other man who had run away with him was found with three gunshot wounds in his stomach—while nailed to the side of a barn with railroad spikes in a rural area thirty miles outside of Boston. The man had been barely alive when discovered. He'd had enough breath left in him to tell the FBI that it had been Ronald Biel who had killed him before dying as he was taken down from the side of the shed.

Having killed a former associate and longtime partner in such a gruesome way, it had been assumed by the FBI—and Avery herself when she had been approached about representing the case after Biel had come to be in custody—that he had simply gone psychotic. It certainly seemed to be the case when the nine bodies he left in his wake after disappearing went unsolved but showed clear signs of Biel's work.

The calling cards of his murders were grotesque. Nails of some form were usually involved. The slitting of throats was also a preferred method. There was always a lot of blood and gore, as if he were purposefully trying to go for the shock factor.

Avery relived each and every one of the cases as she went through the files. The blood, the bodies, the absolute disregard for decency…it made her feel sick.

It made her feel sicker still knowing that he had gotten away from a life sentence due to a technicality. She could have used the technicality to save him from *any* time in prison but had opted not to. She'd rather live with knowing that she purposefully lost a case than knowing that she had helped a psychotic murderer go free.

The technicality had come in the fact that Biel's DNA had not been present at any of the scenes and that one of the scenes had been contaminated by the Boston PD. However, the DNA of Albert Leary, a known mob boss and associate of Biel's, *had* been found at two of the scenes. Even to this day, Leary had never been discovered. It was a Jimmy Hoffa–type mystery. While on trial, even Ronald Biel had said that if Leary was alive, he'd happily claim the murders. Based on Leary's history, the jury had brought this hook, line, and sinker. Leary remained missing and Biel got off with a seven-year sentence—which had been shortened to six due to good behavior, as Avery had recently discovered. Things had gotten so bad by midway through the trial that even the mob was doing everything they could to wash their hands of him.

As she read back over all of this, the door to the small holding room opened up. A man she had met a few times before walked in—William Ackerman, the prison warden. He was accompanied by a security guard who looked like he never smiled and was all business all of the time. Ackerman was dressed in a polo and khakis. He was in his late fifties but had the look of a man still exploring his forties; his hair was barely touched by white and his posture spoke of someone who worked out or, at the very least, had some sort of military background.

"Detective Black," Ackerman said, coming to the table and offering his hand.

Avery stood up, shook the offered hand, and waited to see if the guard would also offer. When it was clear that he would not, Avery gathered up the files.

"Are we all set?" she asked.

"We are. I have spoken to Biel's cellmate, a man by the name of Antoine Evans. He will be in the cell while you are there and I have given him firm instructions to answer any questions you may have. I tell you this because if he gets lippy or straight up rude, he may get roughed up a bit in front of you. So be forewarned."

"That's fine with me," she said. "Lead the way."

Avery followed Ackerman and his guard out of the room, down a small administrative corridor, and then through a set of double doors he opened with his security card. Beyond those doors was the east wing of the prison. Entering into the halls of a maximum security prison was nothing new to her. She had, after all, done it several times when she had come to visit with Howard. But with new blood in the air and a new case that had a sense of urgency to it, something about the prison seemed more primal now.

How did the fact that Howard and Biel were in this place at the same time for several year escape my attention? she wondered as she followed Ackerman. *Had I really pushed Biel that far out of my mind?*

Near the end of the corridor, Ackerman came to a stop. The guard thumped the cell bars with his nightstick. A shape behind the bars moved slowly backward. As Avery stepped forward, she saw a tall, thin black man in the cell. When the guard took out his keys, he looked in to the prisoner and said, "On the bunk, now."

The man did as he was asked, taking a seat on the bunk that was pushed against the left side of the wall. The guard opened the door and stepped inside, followed by Ackerman. Avery went in behind the two men, her eyes instantly going to the other bunk, pushed against the other side of the cell.

"This was Ronald Biel's?" she asked.

"It was," Ackerman said. "And this," he said, nodding to the tall black man, "is Antoine Evans. He was Biel's cellmate for a little over two years."

Wasting no time, Avery focused her attention on Evans. "Biel was released on good behavior," she said, not really caring if Warden Ackerman resented the remark dropped so casually. "Did you ever see any of this so-called good behavior?"

"Yeah," Evans said. "I mean, he was a stand-up dude." He grinned at her in a way that was not quite inappropriate, but made her skin crawl nonetheless.

"Something funny?" she asked.

"Sort of. I've seen you before. I just realized it."

"Sorry to disappoint you," Avery said. "But you and I have never met."

"Nah, not like that. Biel…he…" He stopped here and chuckled. "Warden, if you take the cover off of Biel's bunk, you'll find a tear in the bottom right corner."

Ackerman gave Evans a look of distrust before nudging the guard. The guard went to the vacant bunk, tore the cover and fitted sheet off of it, and examined the bottom right corner.

"He's right," the guard said, fingering the tear in the mattress. "And there's something inside."

Ackerman gave a nod of approval and the guard hesitantly dug deeper into the slit in the mattress. It only took a few seconds. When he pulled his hand back out, there was a large Ziplock bag in his hand. It contained what looked like an assortment of paper. The guard handed the clear baggie to Ackerman. He looked inside for a just a moment, shook his head, and uttered a curse.

"Figures," he said, handing the bag to Avery.

She took it, not quite sure what to expect. She took out one of the pieces of paper and discovered that it was an old newspaper article. It was from three years ago, detailing a drug bust that she had been a part of. Near the top, just under the article title, was a small picture. It showed her, taken from the right side, as she was speaking into a cell phone.

The next piece of paper was from a magazine. It was half of a page, detailing Ronald Biel's case in court. She remembered the article quite clearly as she read it over and looked at the picture; it had been the talk of the town for about a week in the local rags. The picture showed her standing at the bench in the courtroom, giving what the picture showed to be an impassioned plea.

"What the hell is this?" she asked as she kept flipping through the pages and fragments within the bag.

"Man, Ron was obsessed with you," Evans said. "He always said you were a lawyer or something, though. Talked about you all the time. Like he knew you."

"What kind of stuff did he say?"

"That you were smart and beautiful. But he got weird sometimes, too. He'd talk to me about what he thought you might taste like. And not just down there," he said, nodding toward her waist. "But like, the nape of your neck and your fingers. I'd tell him to shut up about it, but he'd go on and on."

"When did he do this?" Ackerman asked.

"I don't know. I mean, pretty recently. Right before he was released, he kept saying he couldn't wait to see you."

"Anything about sexual assault or rape?" Ackerman asked.

Avery shot him an annoyed look. *Of course a man would instantly take it there,* she thought. But she also understood it; the man worked with violent men and psychopaths day in and day out.

"No," Evans said. "In fact, one time when I joked about him jerking it to those pictures at night, he got *mad.* Like, I thought he was going to throw a punch. He didn't talk to me for like a week."

"Did he tell you how he knew me?" Avery asked.

"Just said you were some lawyer lady he had crossed paths with."

"And the entire time you were here, as his cellmate, you never saw a mean streak in him?"

Evans laughed a bit at this and then shrugged. "Look. I know what he was accused of. And really, he's a weird dude—talking about what your fingers taste like and the shape of your pillow when you sleep. So I could always see that part of him. Everyone in here has a mean streak, you know? But with the exception of that one time he got pissed at me for making that joke about your pictures, he was nothing but nice. Real civil to me."

"I hate to say it," Ackerman said. "But you're going to hear more of the same from the guards and the staff. We never had a single issue with him."

As Avery continued to look through the baggie of pictures, she wasn't able to find any comfort in that. Near the back of the collection, she saw that he had even somehow managed to go online and find the picture of her that had once graced the ABOUT US page on the Seymour and Fitch website.

A wave of nausea suddenly passed through her. "In all of his talking, did Biel ever mention where he might be headed when he was released?"

"Not that I remember," Evans said. "All he said for sure that he was going to be sticking around here—that he didn't see the point in moving far. Said a man can't ever outrun his demons, so why tire yourself trying. Or some weird shit like that."

"Thanks," Avery said, suddenly needing to get the hell out of the cell.

She went out with Ackerman right behind her. He could tell that she was shaken up but it was obvious that he wasn't sure how to sympathize.

"You get what you need?" he asked.

It was a tricky question. On the one hand, she had nothing—no idea where Biel was headed or where he might currently be hiding out. Yet on the other hand, she now knew that he had apparently been harboring a long-standing obsession with her.

And it was he who threw the cat, she thought. *He knows where I live.*

A shudder passed through her. Now that she knew with absolute certainty that Biel had her on his mind, she felt almost like she was being hunted.

And it was not a feeling that Avery intended to take lightly.

CHAPTER EIGHTEEN

The moment she got to her car, she looked at the brief notes she had taken while looking over Biel's file inside the prison. Among them was the name and number of the psychiatrist who had met with Biel during and immediately following the trial. She called the number and was handled by a receptionist. After having to use a few choice words and reciting her badge number to the woman on the other end, she was put through to Dr. Janelle Pearson.

When Pearson answered the phone, she sounded livid...but in that quiet and calm sort of way that psychiatrists tended to be well rehearsed in.

"I don't what your issue is," Pearson said, not bothering with introductions or formalities, "but I am currently with a client. This is highly unprofessional and rude."

"I understand that, and I apologize," Avery said. "However, it is quite urgent that I speak with you about Ronald Biel."

There was a shocked silence on the line before Pearson responded. "I've put that behind me. No need to dig it up again. Now, if you—"

"He was released three week ago," Avery said. "And in confidence, I can tell you that I am fairly certain he's picked up where he left off."

"Released?" Pearson said, nearly disgusted. "Already?"

"Yes. Look, Doctor...I'm about twenty minutes away from your office. Can you please push some things around so I can speak with you? I won't take up too much of your time."

Avery was again met with that shocked silence. She could almost hear Dr. Pearson trying to comprehend what Avery had said. Finally, she responded: "Yes, of course."

"I'll see you then," Avery said, hanging up before the conversation got longer or more awkward than it needed to be.

She drove to the address, getting there easily due to the moderate lull in traffic. Being back on a case after two stagnant weeks in a hospital room, she was amazed at how quickly the day seemed to be passing. It was nearing eleven in the morning and although she'd already made three stops—first to see Jane Seymour, then by the now-deceased Mitchell Brennan's residence, and lastly, the prison—she felt like she'd gotten nothing accomplished.

But it felt good to be moving forward—to be working toward something again. The fact that she apparently had a stalker somewhere out there who could place her and her loved ones in jeopardy only enhanced it.

She drove on toward Janelle Pearson's office, her fists white-knuckled with determination as she gripped the steering wheel.

***

When she arrived at the psychiatrist's office, Avery saw that a small placard-type sign had been placed in the glass door. It read: *Unexpected Emergency. Be back in an hour.*

Assuming the emergency was the fact that she was visiting, Avery approached the door and knocked. A woman came to the door right away. She was tall, had short-cropped red hair, and wore a pair of wire-rimmed glasses. Avery showed the woman her badge. The woman on the other side unlocked the door right away and let her in.

"Dr. Pearson?" Avery asked.

"Yes. Sorry I was rude on the phone. It's very uncommon to be interrupted mid-session, though. Fortunately, the client understood."

"And thank *you* for understanding the grave nature of the situation I'm in right now," Avery said.

"Please, come back to my office. I've got a fresh pot of coffee on."

Pearson hurriedly led Avery to the rear of the building. Her office sat in the back and was roughly the size of Avery's apartment. A huge oak desk sat near the far wall, up three carpeted stairs. The rest of the office consisted of a lush couch and a gorgeous armchair. Calming abstract paintings hung on every wall.

"Please, have a seat," Pearson said as she walked over to a miniature coffee bar and set about pouring their coffee.

Avery sat on the couch, not liking how it made her feel as if she were being studied. "So, just to confirm," Avery said, "you *did* evaluate Ronald Biel around the time of his trial, correct?"

"I did. Not that it did any good, mind you."

She had come back to the couch and armchair, handing Avery a cup of coffee and setting a small tray down with packets of sugar and cream. Avery added some sugar, stirred, and sipped.

"Why do you say it didn't do any good?"

"Because by the end of the trial, I think the jurors and the judge had made up their minds. I know that Ronald was never convicted of the actual murders and that was tragic. But even aside from that, there was an energy in the air; everyone wanted him in prison. The jury, the judge, the entire city."

"I'd be in that number as well," Avery said. "I was the attorney representing him. And I admittedly tossed the case."

"I thought your name was familiar when I spoke with you on the phone," Pearson said.

"I take it you didn't think prison was the best place for him?"

"God no. I recommended quite strongly that he be committed to a mental institution. In the end, it all fell on deaf ears."

"Can you tell me exactly why you made that recommendation?" Avery asked.

Pearson drank from her coffee and looked down at the coffee table that sat between them. She stared dimly, as if trying not to recall that time of her life but knowing she needed to.

"Ronald Biel was a terrifying man," she said. "I'm sure you must have sensed some of it, working so closely with him."

Avery nodded. She *had* felt some sort of wrongness about him—an evil that seemed to come off of him in pulses of energy. It's one of the reasons she so easily made the decision to half-ass the case to make sure he was found guilty.

"I don't say that to be dramatic," Pearson said. "I've been in this line of work for eighteen years and I can say without any hesitation that Ronald Biel was one of the most horrific people I have ever met. He all but came out and admitted to committing the murders, but never quite enough for me to go to the police with—and yes, I would have taken the risk of breaking doctor-patient confidentiality in that case. The man had a bloodlust like I had never seen before. He'd talk about things he had seen during the course of his life: gory movies, alleged snuff films, roadkill, a deer he shot as a teenager. He spoke about this stuff the way a scholar would speak about literature or philosophy."

"Certainly that's not enough for someone to be labeled insane, though," Avery said.

"No. But after logging more than forty hours with him, there was more than enough. I can practically recite the list of diagnoses that I sent to the courts. I even considered suggesting that he wasn't fit to stand trial."

"What were some of the diagnoses?" Avery asked.

"On the lighter side of things, he was obsessive compulsive. The man also had a memory like a bank vault. He also clearly had a case of antisocial personality disorder. He lacked empathy or compassion for his fellow man. He showed no remorse. There were several times when I allowed him to sort of free roam during our conversations. I'd ask him what was on his mind that day and he'd up come with some very morbid things. He'd talk about his curiosity concerning the human body. He speculated on how much blood could be lost from a very small wound to the neck, how long it would take to bleed out someone. He talked about some of the things he had seen while in the mob and how he had very badly wanted to be a part of it. We're talking about dismembered bodies, execution-style shootings. He spent a good fifteen minutes during one session telling me what the brain matter of a man that had been shot at point-blank range looked like. He said it was beautiful and inspiring."

"My God. How do you….I mean, how do you think the courts were able to push all of that aside? Surely he needed some sort of clinical help."

"I agree. But while it angered me, I also understand it. You have to think about it through the eyes of the public, Detective. You and I are accustomed to seeing killers and psychopaths through lenses that education and our careers have placed over our eyes. But the public…that's a different creature."

"How so?"

She smirked nervously. "I always use the example of John Wayne Gacy. Horrid serial killer. You know his profile, I assume?"

Avery nodded. She'd done a fake case study on the infamous killer while in college.

"The media has made him out to be this mythical figure over time. But aside from his atrocious crimes, he didn't fit the stark profile of a serial killer—or, at least, what the public thinks a serial killer is supposed to act, look, and behave like. There are many reports about Gacy that state that those who knew him well or even just barely said that he came across as just an average man. Maybe even slightly charming. So when you have a man like Ronald Biel who is not presenting any of the monstrous serial killer tropes the jury is expecting, there's a sort of humanization that occurs. They don't see him as a crazy monster that clearly needs mental help. They seem him as a human…a flawed human capable of monstrous acts. Do you follow me?"

"I do," Avery said thoughtfully.

"And the scary thing about Gacy is this," Pearson said. "After his execution, his brain was removed and examined by a specialist. Do you know what results they found?"

"None," Avery said. "That study showed not a single abnormality."

"That's right," Pearson said. "According to the science of it all and the results of that study, the brain of John Wayne Gacy was just as normal as yours and mine. I'm willing to bet the same is true of Ronald Biel."

"So what you're trying to tell me…" Avery started.

"…is that you need to be careful. Biel, in my estimation, is a normal human with no clear mental breaks—no detachment from reality at all. Yet he is a man of no remorse. He is a man capable of monstrous things. And if he has started killing again after six years away, I can't help but wonder if he has killed off the man and become the monster."

CHAPTER NINETEEN

Her talk with Pearson had Avery feeling scared and jittery—an alarming chain of events, as Avery wasn't someone who spooked easily. With no clear next step, she felt the urgent need to head back to Ramirez's place to make sure Rose was still holding up okay. She was sure her daughter was irritable by now, a prisoner of her mother's mess and having to put her life on hold. Of course, in the process, her life was likely being saved but Avery didn't expect Rose to quite understand and appreciate that just yet.

The drive to Ramirez's place took about forty minutes because of the congested flow of lunch-hour traffic. She wondered who was currently on surveillance detail and thought about being bold and driving out in front of the place just to see. But in the end, she stuck with the safer route. She parked behind the building and then entered along the side. The side door led to the elevators and the building's small laundry room.

As she took the elevator up to Ramirez's apartment, she considered calling Connelly, just to give him an update. She then thought better of it, not wanting to poke at the bear until there was just reason to.

Avery stepped off on the third floor and walked halfway down to the hall to Ramirez's door. She slipped her key in the lock and turned it. She also called out to Rose at the same time, not wanting to alarm her.

"Rose? It's just me."

She pushed the door, stepping inside and realizing only then that there had been no resistance at all when she had unlocked the door. *It was already unlocked,* she thought.

She took two steps into the apartment and her heart leaped up into her throat. A chill raced through her as she drew her Glock.

The place was trashed.

Couch cushions were strewn everywhere. A few wine glasses from the kitchen had been shattered against the living room wall. The refrigerator door was open; milk, tea, and juice were puddled on the floor. Pictures and their frames were all over the floor.

"Rose!"

The sound of her screaming her daughter's name filled the place like a boom of thunder. As she stalked into the living room, her gun drawn and ready to fire at a moment's notice, she took in more of the destruction. DVDs were scattered all over the living room. A large hole had been punched into the screen of the television.

And still, she had heard nothing from Rose.

She checked behind the kitchen counters and bar to make sure the area was clear before moving on to the bedroom. The door was mostly closed so she kicked it and went rushing in, certain that someone was there on the other side.

But there was no one.

She *did* see something that made her go cold again, though.

There was a message on the bedroom wall, centered directly over the bed. From what she could tell, it had been written in magic marker. The handwriting appeared to be the same as the note on the cat and the dummy in the warehouse. The message read: **ONE BY ONE, EVERYONE YOU LOVE. THEN JUST YOU AND I.**

Rose.

Her heart broke to think that Biel had come here and taken Rose. But how had he gotten by police surveillance? How had he—

She interrupted her own thoughts as she pulled out her cell phone. Her hands were trembling and there was a sob welling up in her throat. She was going to call O'Malley to see who the hell had been stationed as lookout. And God help whoever it was.

But before she could place the call, she heard a noise from the living room.

Her teeth gritting and her fingers wanting something to give her a reason to fire, Avery went quickly and quietly to the doorway's edge between the bedroom and living room.

The front door was creaking open. Hesitant footsteps shuffled forward. Avery readied herself to spring, still struggling down a sob. She kept repeating Rose's name in her head like a mantra while she thought of the deplorable things she would do to Biel when she caught him.

But then she heard another noise that dashed all of those thoughts.

Rose's voice, coming from the living room.

"Mom?"

There was fear and panic in her voice but even so, it was the sweetest sound Avery could ever remember hearing in her life. She finally let the sob out, holstered her sidearm, and went running into the living room.

Rose was frozen a few steps inside the entryway, taking the state of the apartment in with a horrified expression.

"Rose," Avery said in a whisper, running to her daughter and taking her in her arms.

"Mom…what the hell happened?"

"I thought you were gone," she said. "I thought he had taken you…"

"No…Mom, my God. Is it this serious now?"

Avery nodded, not yet comfortable enough to let Rose go. She hugged her tight, perhaps as tight as she ever had. When she finally felt at peace, she released Rose and took a step back to give her daughter some space.

"Where were you?" she asked.

"I left here like an hour and a half ago," she said. "Sawyer and Dennison gave me a lift over to my place. I needed some new clothes. I took a shower, made a few eggs. Jesus, Mom…this place was not like this when I left."

Avery nodded, trying to determine what it meant. Had Biel known Rose and the surveillance had been gone so he made his break-in in their absence? Or had he come here hoping for Rose to be home so he could take her? Or kill her…

"So what are we supposed to do now?" Rose asked.

Avery wanted very badly to provide Rose with a comforting response but in that moment, she simply could not find the right words.

***

Avery mostly stood aside in a state of shock while Sawyer and Dennison looked the apartment over. Avery knew that O'Malley was on the way but she didn't think it would matter. Biel clearly had no worries about being caught. It was almost like he had her movements mapped out. She felt sure that a police presence around Ramirez's place so soon after he had entered would not bother him in the least. Hell, he had probably moved on by now to taunt her some other way.

She stepped into the bedroom and looked at the note scrawled over Ramirez's bed again. *One by one, everyone you love. Then just you and I.*

It was broken down in terms of lines to resemble a poem on a page. And hell, even the phrasing and breaking of the words felt and sounded like a poem.

As she looked at the message, Rose came to the doorway. She no longer looked terrified but she looked tired. This whole ordeal had certainly taken it out of her.

"You're a trouper, kid," Avery said.

"Well, I'm a scared trouper," Rose said. "And, quite frankly, a pissed off trouper, too."

"I know," Avery said. "And I'm sorry. But I honestly don't know what else to do."

"They're going to move us again, aren't they?" Rose asked.

"Probably."

"I have a life, Mom. You know that, right?"

"I do. And by trying to keep you safe right now, I'm trying to make sure that life is not in danger. You know *that,* right?"

Rose only nodded as she looked at the message on the wall.

"You think he was coming for me or did he know I was gone?"

Eerie how much she thinks like me, Avery thought. "I don't know yet," she answered honestly. "But either way, I'm sure he enjoys knowing that he has us on the run."

"Are you working on it?" Rose asked. "Are they letting you on the case?"

"As of this morning, yes."

"Then catch the fucker already," Rose said. She couldn't suppress the small smile that touched the corner of her lips.

The tense yet somehow bonding moment was interrupted by O'Malley's voice. It came from the living room like a bullhorn.

"Black?"

"In here," she called back.

O'Malley came into the room, looked around, and settled his eyes on the message scrawled on the wall. "This is bad, Black."

"I know."

"And it gets worse," O'Malley said. "I got a call literally as I was coming into the building. We've got another body. Don't know for sure if it's linked to Biel or not, but it's looking like it."

"How do you know?"

"Because it's someone you know. Someone you spoke with recently. Black…Jane Seymour has been murdered."

CHAPTER TWENTY

Avery wished, at the very least, they could move the car. As it was, it was parked facing the street and the afternoon sun was beating directly down on her, the car, and the dead woman inside. But moving the car would risk contaminating the crime scene so they had to make do with what they had.

Jane Seymour's car was parked to the far side of the Seymour and Fitch lot. The only other cars in the lot belonged to one of the other attorneys and the young receptionist Avery had spoken to not even seven hours ago. That receptionist, a woman by the name of Amy Wright, was inside with Finley as he took her statement. Avery had already spoken to her and learned how she had seen Jane come back from her late lunch, watching as she parked her car out of sight of the front doors. When ten minutes passed and Jane had not come inside, Amy had gone out to see if she needed anything.

What she had found was Jane tied to her front seat with bailing wire. Her throat had been slit from ear to ear, the blood from which had coated the windshield, dashboard, and front seat. There were also two stab wounds in her chest, one of which Avery was pretty sure had landed directly in her heart.

The loss of Jane hurt. Even though working for her seemed like it had been just a blip on the radar years ago, Avery could not ignore the fact that it had been her first real job. And it had done wonders for her financially and professionally. Jane had taken a chance by hiring her and had become a mentor and friend.

And now Avery was having to view her as just another dead body—another victim. All the blood, the dead eyes, her mouth just slightly agape and her eyes wide open in shock, seeing absolutely nothing.

It was starting to feel personal now. Maybe even more dangerous than it had earlier in the day.

Avery and O'Malley had gathered all the information there was to have—and it wasn't much at all.

The other attorney had seen nothing. He had gone running outside to see what was wrong with Amy when she had started screaming. He'd not been able to look at more than the dark red stains on the windshield and had not come back out of the building since.

95

"The psycho is dedicated as hell, I'll give him that much," O'Malley said. "So give the rundown. When were you here?"

"Right around nine o'clock," Avery said. "No later than nine thirty."

"And Amy Wright says she's pretty sure Jane left for lunch sometime around twelve thirty. She wasn't sure when she saw Amy's car pull back in, but she's pretty sure it couldn't have been later than one forty-five. I checked with dispatch and that all lines up; the call came in at one fifty-one. So let's round that up to two o'clock. We're talking five hours—five hours from the time you met with Jane to the moment she died. He was watching you the whole time, Avery."

She was pretty sure she detected a hint of annoyance in his voice. He seemed to be asking her how she'd not noticed someone following her or spying on her. She supposed he had a point but at the same time, it pissed her off.

"The question remains, though," Avery said. "Did he kill Jane because she was connected to his prison sentence or did he kill her because he wants to prove a point to me?"

"What kind of a point?" O'Malley asked.

"That he knows where I've been. That he can strike anyone at any time. He proved it in Ramirez's apartment at some point this morning and he proved it with Amy. It feels like he's teasing me. Like he could take me whenever he wanted."

"It's pretty clear that he's out for vengeance," O'Malley said.

"You think this is proof enough for Connelly to drop the Howard Randall thing?"

"Maybe. But the fact the idiot actually had the nerve to jump you yesterday is not sitting well with him."

There was another unspoken accusation there, one she felt quite personally. *I was jumped by Howard yesterday and never saw it coming. Biel is apparently stalking me, knowing where I've been and where I'm headed. Maybe I* am *off of my game. Am I being too distracted by Ramirez?*

She shook the thought away.

To hell with that, she thought. *This bastard is mine.*

"So let's say Biel *is* closing in on you," O'Malley said. "We've got Rose under constant surveillance. Three officers are on her at all times now, as you know. She's at the station right now as Connelly is trying to figure out where to put you."

"I'm not homeless," she said, a little resentfully.

"Sorry, Avery. But for right now, you sort of are. Anyway…he won't get to Rose. So who else from that time in your life, back when you were an attorney, would he go after next?"

She thought hard about it. Rose came to mind, of course, but she was safe and under police protection. She ran through the memories of the trial and thought of a moment when Biel had been coming into the courtroom. He had sat down and leaned in close to Avery, whispering something.

Jack had been there. Sitting behind them, there to cheer her on during this huge case that could really put her on the map. And when Biel had whispered to her, just a jeering sort of comment about the trial, Jack had stepped forward. She couldn't remember what he had said but it had caused Biel to stare him down with those evil eyes of his.

He'd said nothing—just started whistling that damned song.

The answer unfolded like this in her head. And although it seemed like a long shot, Biel was showing them that he was not holding back.

"Jack," she finally answered.

"Who's that?" O'Malley asked.

"My ex-husband," she said. And now that she had said his name and had had a few seconds to think it over, it *did* seem like a logical step somewhere in Biel's sick progression. She pulled out her phone, turned away from the grisly scene in Jane Seymour's front seat, and placed a call to Jack. She was pretty sure it was the first time she had called him in at least nine months—and even then, it had been to share information about Rose.

The phone rang. Then it rang again and again and a fourth time before Jack's voice mail picked up. Sure, he could simply be dodging her calls (it wouldn't be the first time) but given the circumstances, that wasn't a risk she was going to take.

"No answer," she said, ending the call.

"You going to go over there?"

"Yeah," she said. "It'll take about half an hour. Do me a favor and make absolutely certain that Rose stays at the precinct until I get back there. I want *you* personally in charge of that."

O'Malley gave a reluctant nod. He clearly didn't want to be held liable for such a responsibility but he also knew that Avery would not take no for an answer. Satisfied that he would hold his word, Avery hurried to her car. Before she got in, she took one final look back at Jane. The reality of her death had not quite sunk in. She'd just seen her five hours ago and there were so many memories of working with her floating through her head.

She felt sorrow welling up in her heart but she pushed it away. She pushed it aside into another part of her heart, a place where she could already feel it festering into something that had the familiar barbs and bruises of anger.

CHAPTER TWENTY ONE

Avery had only ever been to Jack's house out in Waltham a single time before, and that had only been to give Rose a ride over. She had not stepped inside, nor had she had any desire to do so. The neighborhood was quiet, especially at 3:00 in the afternoon. It was a cute place to live, with thin clean sidewalks for kids to learn to drive their bikes, small yards with just enough space for cute landscaping. The houses were nice yet modest. It was just the kind of place she'd expected Jack to move to after the divorce. He'd stayed in the city up until a year and a half ago, moving out here to a smaller place to live as a forty-something bachelor who had just started to learn to make a real living working from home as a copy editor for a few online magazines.

She parked in front of his house, already rolling her eyes at what she expected to find. She knew the place would be clean; Jack was nothing if not a neat freak. But she also knew that he was quite lazy and still something of a child. She walked up the porch steps, fully expecting to find him sitting at some pretentious desk, typing away with a beer at his side. She wondered if he still started drinking at one in the afternoon when it was an option.

Good for him, she thought as she approached the door. *I truly hope he's finally happy.*

She knocked on the door but got no answer. She looked along the edge of the doorframe and saw where there *should* be a doorbell. But the slot was empty. She shook her head. Of course it was. If the one that was here before broke, Jack would put it off for as long as he could—forever if at all possible.

"Jack?" she asked, not quite shouting but raising her voice.

She knocked on the door again, starting to worry. She knocked harder this time, hard enough to sting her knuckles. As she waited for an answer, she thought of the scene at Mitch Brennan's house and of what Jane Seymour's call had looked like. Both of those murders had occurred within at least twelve hours of each other.

Biel's not fucking around, she thought. *He could have easily been out here to visit Jack between killing Brennan and Jane.*

"Jack?" she said. She tried to be louder than last time, but it came out in a croak of sorts.

To hell with it, she thought.

99

She drew her Glock, took a step back, and then threw her leg up. Her follow-thorough was nice and fluid. She connected squarely with the door, just beneath the door knob, and the door buckled a bit before finally swinging in. The lock in the frame busted, but it would be easy to repair—as easy as the missing doorbell, she thought with scared humor.

The place was quiet. Eerily so. Right away, she knew she was right. Biel had already been here. She'd find Jack dead. She knew he was home because she'd seen his car in the driveway, parked outside of the garage and not in it because he thought the idea of garages was stupid and overly American.

"A little house for a car," he'd joked one time. *"How spoiled are we as a country anyway?"*

"Jack?"

She got no answer again but this time she *did* hear something. There was the thumping of some sort of bass from music being played upstairs. At first, she felt relief at this sound but then remembered seeing the television on at the Brennan residence.

The music was pretty loud. If Biel had managed to get into the house and the music had been that loud, Jack would have never heard him.

She hurried through the living room, not allowing herself the time or freedom to look at the place. All she could tell was that it was indeed very clean and well cared for. As she went through the living room and into a small hallway between the living room and kitchen, she saw two rooms at the end of the hall and a stairway that came before either of them.

Gun still drawn, she slowly made her way up the stairs. The music was louder than she'd first thought, the bass driving and consistent. By the time she reached the top of the stairs, she recognized it as a Massive Attack song. She couldn't help but think that of course Jack still listened to that type of music. She'd loved it at one time, too, but age had kicked in and she now settled for whatever was on the radio.

She came up to the hallway, again making herself ignore the rest of the place. No time to take in how well Jack was doing these days. She had to get to the bedroom to be sure—to see if her fear (which was now becoming a certainty) was true.

The music was blasting from the last room along the hallway. The door was cracked open. As she quietly hurried toward the door, her palms sweating and the Glock still gripped tightly in her hands, the song reached a quiet moment, a drop between chorus and bridge, and she heard a groan.

A man, and he sounded like he was in pain.

Hurt, she thought, *but at least he's still alive…*

She came to the door, reached out, and eased it open. The music seeped out, like the soundtrack to a past with the man she was sure she'd find injured and bleeding on the floor.

But that's not what she saw. Not even close. It took her a full two seconds to understand what she was seeing, but by then things had already taken a turn for the worst.

Jack was standing up, completely naked beside his desk. Between Jack and the desk there was a woman with long blonde hair, bent over with her backside to Jack. She was also naked. They were in perfect sync, working in rhythm together. The woman moaned and it was drowned out by the music. Jack groaned again in response.

The woman tossed her head to the side to get her gorgeous hair out of her face.

And that's when she spotted Avery standing in the doorway.

"What the *fuck*?" she yelled as she pulled away from Jack.

Jack was too dazed and still lustfully lost in the moment to gather what was going on right away. Yet as he took in his partner, spooked, angry, and embarrassed, he also turned to the doorway.

"Avery? What the hell…?"

"Jesus…" Avery said, stepping out of the doorway. "Jack, I'm so sorry. But trust me…I have a good explanation!"

The woman was yelling again, mostly drowned out by the music. The music was then cut off and it was all too clear. The woman was apparently not mad at Jack for the sudden appearance of his ex-wife; she was mad at his ex-wife for interrupting their afternoon delight.

It took a full minute or so before the woman came storming out of the room. She was fully dressed and got in Avery's face. She was clearly livid but as she looked into Avery's eyes, something in her fury dropped. The woman, who was easily no older than thirty, could see in Avery's eyes that this was not a fight she wanted to start.

Avery smiled at her and nodded. "You'll have him back in ten minutes," she said. "You can wait downstairs for all I care."

The girl looked away and walked down the stairs slowly, as if confused and maybe even a little scared.

Avery turned back into the room just in time to see Jack pulling on his shirt. When it was over his head, he looked at her with a mix of anger and amusement.

"So what the hell is going on?" Jack said. "My first thought was that maybe something was wrong with Rose. But…Avery…you had your gun out. What gives?"

"I had to talk to you."

"Then use the phone."

"I did. I called and you didn't answer. I also knocked on the door and called out your name. Clearly, you were too preoccupied to hear either."

"Are you seriously going to give me shit for having sex in my house in the middle of the afternoon?"

"No," she said. She had to bite back a remark that was dancing on her tongue: *How old is she, anyway? At least fifteen years younger than you, right?*

"Rose is okay?" Jack asked.

"Rose is fine. There's something else…some trouble, I think. And I had to make sure you were okay."

"I'm not in any trouble," Jack said. "Things are going good, actually. Work is going well, I've been with Tricia for about three months now," he said, nodding toward the door.

"That's great," she said. "But I really didn't come by to catch up, Jack. Look…do you remember me working a case with a guy named Ronald Biel?"

He didn't have to think for long before he nodded. "Yeah. The mob guy. Sick piece of shit, right? He whispered something in your ear at the trial and I got in his face a little."

It's eerie how well he remembers things like that, she thought. *Then again, he* did *always put me first. He supported me when I put work over him…*

No need to go there, some other, wiser part of her spoke up.

"Right," she said. "Well, he was released three weeks ago. And we're pretty sure he's killed at least three people so far. One was his probation officer from back then. Another was an attorney I worked with—Jane Seymour."

"Shit," he said. "I remember Jane. My God. When did this happen?"

"Jane was killed about three hours ago as far as we can tell. But beyond that, Biel is also threatening me. There have been letters, vandalism, maybe stalking. I don't know. He wrecked an apartment that Rose and I were hiding out in and—"

"Rose is caught up in this? What the hell have you done, Avery?"

"I've done nothing."

"She needs to be with me if this psycho is after you," Jack said. "She'd be safer."

It's not a wrong thought, she said. *But I'll be damned if he's going to try to blame this on me.*

"Not right now."

"Um, hell yes right now. Avery, you can't just…"

He trailed off here, not sure where to go with it.

"I thought of that…of bringing her here," Avery admitted. "But honestly, I don't know if she *would* be safer here. He's made it clear that he's going to come after me and the people I love. He's also killing people that were close to the case and close to me back during the case. We were married then, Jack. And I think he might have you on his list. If he *does,* then Rose is much safer with me, under police protection."

"This is ridiculous," he said. "You really mean to tell me that there's a killer out there that might be gunning for me because I used to be involved with you?"

"Potentially, yes."

"That's just perfect," Jack said. "You're managing to screw up my life even when you're not a part of it."

And there's another typical Jack response. Focusing on a past hurt and how it defined him rather than how he can make things better right now, in the moment. A little selfish, but given the circumstances, it's understandable.

"I don't care how you feel about me, Jack. But I do care about Rose having a father. I care about her well-being. So I need to ask that you go somewhere else. Get a hotel room. You and Tricia can finish what I interrupted."

It was immature and she knew it, but it felt rather good to let the remark out. Jack, on the other hand, didn't even seem to notice. He was too irritated that Avery had the audacity to think that she could give him orders.

"I'm not going to go live in a hotel based on some wild assumption you have," he said.

"It's a little more than just an assumption," she said.

"Whatever. I don't jump when you say so anymore, Avery. That didn't really work for us last time either, did it?"

"Don't do it for me, then," Avery said. "Do it for Rose."

"Don't you dare use her as some sort of lure to get me to bite into your little theories. Forget it, Avery. I appreciate the concern— I guess—but no, I'm not leaving."

"You stubborn asshole," she said in a shout. "This is not about me and you. This is about our daughter having a father. Biel is out there and he *is* killing. He's taking out people in my orbit. He killed Jane less than five hours after I spoke with her this morning. The creep threw a dead cat through my window while Rose was with me. Do you get it?"

He slammed his fist down on the table that, less than ten minutes ago, had served as a support for afternoon sex.

"Fine. I'll do it. I'll talk to Tricia and see if I can stay at her place."

"Thank you. And don't use your car. Ride together, in her car. Just in case."

He gave a sarcastic chuckle. "You and your damn orders. Anything else you think I should be doing in the next few days, *Detective*?"

She let the jab go as she turned for the doorway to make her exit. "Yes," she said. "Fix your doorbell." And then, as she made her way out of the room, she added: "And you might want to fix your door, too."

CHAPTER TWENTY TWO

Seeing Jane Seymour's freshly killed body and having to confront Jack all in the span of two hours had taken its toll on Avery. She left Jack's house (not bothering to give Trisha even the slightest of glances on her way out) and headed back into the city. Before she was even off of Jack's street, she realized that she had nowhere to go. Maybe O'Malley had been right: maybe she *was* temporarily homeless.

She called O'Malley and he answered right away. "How's Jack?" he asked.

"Alive. And having a very fun afternoon, I might add. How are things on your end?"

"We've got a section of the city blocked off—a six-block radius, with Seymour and Fitch in the center. But it's not looking good. This guy works fast. We *did* find some sort of fluid on the headrest of Jane's car, though. Probably saliva. The working theory is that as Jane parked her car, Biel approached quickly from nearby, maybe behind the building, and got into the back as she started to get out. Maybe he drooled a bit when he was cutting her up from behind. We're checking on it. Should have results in the next twelve hours or so."

"Sounds good. Any news on where Rose and I are staying?"

"Yeah," O'Malley said. "And I don't think you're going to like it."

***

Avery pulled her car into one of the many vacant spots in the Weston Motel forty minutes later. It was 4:17 and the place was basically dead with the notable exception of three police cars and a few sad-looking cars scattered around the lot. The Weston Motel was not the type of place you went for a good night's rest. Avery knew for a fact that it had once been a hot spot for heroin deals and prostitutes. In the last few years it had managed to drop that reputation but it also wasn't anywhere near a five-star resort—or a four-star. It might scrape the bottom of a third-star rating, and that was being kind. It was a crummy little place tucked away like some forgotten blemish not too far away from Franklin Park.

As she got out of her car, she saw Finley coming out of one of the rooms. He gave her an apologetic grin and then shrugged his shoulders. She met him on the concrete walkway that connected all of the rooms to the main office, the drink machines, and the ice machine.

"If it helps, I argued for something a little nicer," Finley said.

She sighed. "Thanks. But I know how this works. It makes sense. The place is only one level. It's located in an area of town where if most people see a police car, they're not going to cause any trouble. It's a smart move. Where's Rose?"

"Room twelve," Finley said. "And man, is she *pissed*."

"Thanks, Finley," she said as she made her way farther down the concrete walkway toward room twelve.

When she knocked on the door, it was answered right away by Officer Dennison. He smiled at her out of obligation and then stepped aside to let her in. She saw Rose sitting on the bed, scrolling through her phone. The TV was also on but was being mostly ignored.

"You okay, Rose?" she asked.

"No. This sucks."

Dennison chuckle and agreed. "It does suck. But we just ordered pizza."

"Is it just you?" Avery asked.

"No. Sawyer's out in the car. We'll switch in about two or three hours. We're on until midnight and then Dabney and Parks will come in to relieve us."

"That's not necessary," Avery said. "I'm here now. You guys don't need to stay here to protect us."

"Yeah, I know that, and Sawyer knows that. But Connelly doesn't. Or maybe he does, but just wants to be safe."

"Wow, it *does* suck for you, too, huh?"

Dennison laughed at this and Avery was glad to see Rose smile at the sound of the man's raucous laughter. She sat down by Rose on the edge of the bed. When Rose looked up at her, Avery did her best to look her in the eyes—something Rose had never been a fan of.

"I'm sorry," she said. "But I am working as hard as I can to catch him. And when we do, this will all be over."

"I know," Rose said, clearly having to push her frustration aside to be civil. "You saw Dad, I hear? How is he?"

"Oh, he's fine. I convinced him to lay low somewhere else until it all blows over, too."

"Good," Rose said, then returning her attention back to her screen.

Avery decided to leave well enough alone and not push Rose any further. When she was ready to talk, she'd talk. So instead of pestering her daughter further, Avery figured she'd try to be productive. And she'd start by going over the files on Ronald Biel again. Maybe there was something she was missing, something she could closely link to today's two murders.

She went out to her car to retrieve them. She spotted Sawyer in the patrol car parked to the left of room twelve and gave him a little wave. He returned with a shrug and the same apologetic look Finley had given her moments ago.

She unlocked her trunk and took out the small box of files she accumulated between the A1, the prison, Jane, and her own personal files. As she shuffled the box out, Finley was there to shut the trunk for her.

"Need help?" he asked.

"No, I got it," she said. Finley nodded, but followed her all the same.

As she carried the files back to the room, she heard her phone ding from inside her coat pocket, indicating that she'd gotten a text.

O'Malley, she thought. *Maybe they found something else to go by in Jane's car.*

She reached the room, set the files down on the second bed, and fished her phone out of her pocket. She saw right away that the text was not from O'Malley.

It was from a number she didn't know. She was pretty sure she had never seen it before. It read: **I figured I'd be polite and not jump you again. I have a clue for you, since it seems our man is working very quickly. Want the clue? Meet me at your apartment building. 6 p.m. Out back. Come alone. Ooh. Bad reception. Gotta Go. ☺**

Howard, she thought.

Oddly enough, it was the smiley face that sealed the deal. And, of course, he was offering a clue but had left something of a riddle in the message. *Bad reception. That's some sort of clue, too. I know that miserable bastard far too well.*

"You okay?" Finley asked.

"Yeah, I'm good," she said. But she angled herself away from Finley so he couldn't see the message and read it again.

Maybe it's not Howard, she thought. *Maybe it's Biel. Whichever it is, they're probably messaging me from a burner phone. I'd waste my time trying to track it down. And I don't have time to waste with the speed Biel is working.*

And with that thought, she made her decision.

She didn't care if it was Howard or Biel. She'd be happy to meet with either one.

She looked at Rose, still scrolling listlessly on her phone. Making such a reckless decision while in the presence of her daughter felt wrong. But she didn't see where she had any choice.

Six p.m. I'd have to leave in about an hour and twenty minutes. What to do until then?

She looked to the box of files but not for very long. She then looked again at Rose and, slowly, sat back down on the bed. She grabbed the remote from the bedside table and found a rerun of *Friends.* Hearing the laugh track broke Rose from her phone hypnosis and just like that, Avery was spending time with her daughter.

It felt lazy and forced, but it warmed Avery's heart.

And it also made her more certain than ever that she'd be following up on the message she'd just received. Whatever it took to free Rose of this prison she had created, she was willing to do it—even if it meant carelessly risking her own life.

CHAPTER TWENTY THREE

When Avery left the Weston Motel, Rose didn't seem to have any particular feelings about it. It was some of the moody elements of her teenage self, clinging on to a fast-approaching twenty, but that was fine with Avery. She'd rather Rose be detached and moody than clingy and panicked as her mother went speeding off to her next dangerous location.

The message had said to show up alone, so she had remained mum on her location when Sawyer and Dennison had asked her. *"Just checking out a possible lead,"* she had said.

And that had been that.

She pulled up behind her apartment building at 5:56, a little shocked by how alien the place felt to her now. It had been a hectic two weeks, filled with dark emotions she had still not yet dealt with. Just because Ramirez was back among the land of the living did not make those feelings go away.

Although she was a few minutes early, she was pretty sure she spotted Howard's little clue within his text message right away.

Ooh, bad reception...

A white van was parked in the far corner of the rear lot of her apartment building. It looked a little worn with age. The lettering along the side was basic—white with simple block lettering. Like the rest of the van, the lettering was worse for wear, yet still readable: HUDSON ELECTRONICS REPAIR – *Specializing in TVs.*

She was hard pressed to remember the last time she'd seen any van—or any *business* for that matter—that boasted about specializing in television repair. Was that even a thing anymore?

Not wanting to tempt Howard, she waited until her phone read 6:00 before she stepped out of her car. She was very aware that he could be somewhere nearby, watching her. It was difficult not to call out to him. But if this was some game he was playing, she figured she needed to play by his rules. Every clue or riddle he had given her in the past had always led to something helpful. Why would this time be any different?

She walked to the van and the closer she got, the more she started to see it as some sort of relic out of time. She could easily imagine Howard having this van stored away somewhere, or maybe he purchased it recently for this very reason. Whatever the case, the van had clearly not seen any real road time in several years.

She tried the door on the back of the van and found it locked. She then tried the driver's side door and it opened without any trouble. She slowly climbed in, taking a glance over her shoulder. There were two people walking down the street at the edge of the block, but they were paying her no attention. If Howard Randall was in the vicinity, he was not showing himself.

The van smelled of dust and mildew yet looked to have recently been tidied up. There was nothing of note in the front seats or on the dashboard. However, when she checked the glove compartment, she found a plastic bag. She slowly pulled it out and inside found something she had not been expecting—something that made her pause and actually laugh out loud.

There were several magnetized letters in the bag, the kind that preschoolers used on refrigerators while learning their ABCs. She looked through them and saw that it was not the entire alphabet, though. Also, there were some letters that were represented two and three times.

At the bottom of the bag was a handwritten note. In stylish cursive, written in pencil, was a question: *What's in a name?*

She observed the handwriting and was quite certain it was not Biel's. Biel's had an almost childlike flare to it. This handwriting was rather elegant and beautiful.

Avery looked to the back of the van. It had been completely cleared out. Aside from some dust and grime, the back of the van was empty. On the left-hand wall, she saw an area that seemed to be much cleaner than the rest of the interior. She hunched over and crawled into the back of the van with the bag in hand. She placed her nose against the cleaner area and smelled something like window cleaner. It had been cleaned recently, while the rest of the van hadn't.

She saw right away what Howard was doing and it made her feel as if he were talking down to her in a way. He was not only providing a clue, but also revealing the steps she needed to take in order to get to it. He was making everything abundantly clear to her, like a parent leaving a kid home alone for the first time.

The magnet letters. The square-shaped clean area in the back of the van. The note, asking *what's in a name?*

Feeling a little foolish, she dumped the magnetized letters out into the floor. Then, on her hands and knees, she started sorting through them. She sorted the vowels out and set them to their own pile and then placed the every R, S, T, and N that she could find in another pile, as they were traditionally the most used letters in the English language.

She started placing the letters on the wall of the van, starting with consonants and trying to come up with a name that she might recognize. As she worked, she found an odd sort of appreciation for what Howard was having her do. In this silly little way, he was making her work for information rather than just leaving the name in a note…or even just sending it directly to her in the text message. While it was wasting her time, it was also keeping her sharp and driven.

She scrambled the letters here and there and kept finding herself drawn to the K. It was a letter that was typically either at the front or the very end of a first name. She tried the K with several vowel formations but had trouble with the consonants that followed. She worked fast, using her love of crosswords and other word puzzles to her advantage.

It took her a little less than two minutes before she figured out the first name, tied into place by the V—which was an oddball letter among the remaining magnets. She looked at it for a moment as she had it unscrambled.

Kevin.

She then looked to the remaining letters and tried sorting them out in a way that made some kind of sense. There were only two vowels remaining out of seven letters, which made it a little easier, but still complicated. After another few minutes, though, it was the inclusion of the S and H magnets that keyed her into it. She'd been trying to cram them into the middle of the last name but then realized that they needed to go at the end…before the two Rs, which were doubled, one behind the other.

With the name spelled out, she stared at it for a moment. She knew who it was but had never even thought about him ever since she'd discovered that Biel had been released. This guy had not even popped up on her radar—mainly because he had no reason to.

Kevin Parrish.

It was a name that had come up a few times during Biel's trial—some former mob flunky who had taken the stand and yielded no results. But he had been the one person Biel had identified as a true friend—which was ironic, as he had tried to kill him during his little nine-victim rampage. If Avery was remembering correctly, she was pretty sure Kevin Parrish had been left without two fingers on his right hand and only one eye.

Given the six years or more than had passed since Biel went to prison, and the mob's tendency not to rat out their own in any way, she didn't know if going to speak with Parrish would be worth her time. If it was a long way to travel, she'd rule him out.

But Howard seems to think he's important, Avery thought. And really, that was good enough for her.

That's when it occurred to her. She'd been thinking this entire time that it seemed strange that Howard would escape from prison. But maybe—juts maybe—he had not escaped out of his own selfish ambitions. Maybe he knew about Biel's release and had escaped in an effort to save her.

The thought was jarring to say the least. Not allowing herself to get sidetracked by it, she pulled out her phone and called up O'Malley. As usual, he answered right away.

"How quickly can you get me an address?" she asked.

"If it concerns the Biel case, then I'll have it for you in five minutes."

"Good. I need the address for Kevin Parrish. Two r's."

"Got it. I'll get right back to you."

They ended the call and Avery let herself out of the van. She looked back at it before heading back for her car. She wondered how long Howard had hidden it away or, more realistically, how recently he had stolen it. The man's mind worked like a computer, thinking quickly and often very far ahead of those he was around.

As she opened her car door, her cell phone buzzed. She saw that O'Malley had already gotten her the address, only three minutes after she'd made the request. *If only they worked this quickly all the time,* she thought.

She read the address and smiled in spite of herself. She wondered if Howard had already known what she was reading.

Kevin Parrish still lived in Boston. More than that, his address was only about fifteen minutes away. It seemed flimsy, but Avery was comfortable feeling that this was a break…finally.

She pulled out of the lot and left the apartment building behind, along with the sense that the place had never really felt like home.

CHAPTER TWENTY FOUR

One thing Avery always appreciated about her job was that she never quite knew what to expect. Even when cases seemed very similar, no two days or two leads were ever the same. She was reminded of this when she pulled up in front of Kevin Parrish's townhouse. He lived in a fairly nice little townhouse complex; each structure contained six to eight townhouses, each boasting their own quaint little front stoop.

She saw Kevin Parrish right away, sitting under his stoop. He was sitting in a rocking chair, smoking a cigarette and reading a book. She could barely remember what he had looked like on the stand during Biel's trial but she was quite sure he did not look like he did as she got out of the car and approached his front stoop.

He had grown his hair long and had one of those beards that Rose sometimes referred to as hipster beards—the sort that needed a good grooming. On Parrish's face, the beard was mostly gray. Avery figured he had to be in his early fifties now. And despite the hair and the unruly beard, the thing that drew Avery's attention more than anything else was the eye patch he wore where his left eye used to be.

She approached the stoop quietly, not wanting to alarm him as he was apparently lost in his book—one of Jesse Ventura's conspiracy titles. She hated to cast stereotypes, but the title seemed to fit the new appearance Parrish had taken on.

"Kevin Parrish?" she asked as she reached the front of his stoop.

He looked up through a cloud of cigarette smoke, setting the book down on his knee. "Yeah, that's me. Who's asking?"

"I'm Detective Avery Black. I'm on some urgent business and I was hoping you'd be able to speak to me about Ronald Biel."

"That's fine," he said with a smirk. "Let's just hope the conversation begins with you giving me the news that he's dead and rotting in a ditch somewhere."

"No, I'm afraid not. In fact, he was released from prison a little over three weeks ago. And since then, it appears that he has killed at least three people. And he's also threatening me and my family."

"How was that asshole not thrown under the prison?" Parrish asked. He punctuated the question by taking a long drag off of his cigarette and then stubbing it out in an ashtray on the porch railing.

"Lots of variables," she said. It was clear that he did not recognize her. And why would he? While she *had* questioned him when he was on the stand, she had not pressed hard. By that point in the proceedings, she had decided to throw the case.

"So he's out there again? As crazy as ever?"

"He is," Avery said. She was a little surprised by his *whatever* sort of attitude. Now that she was thinking about it, she wondered if Kevin Parrish might be somewhere on Biel's list of people to kill.

"So what do you need from me?" he asked.

"First and foremost, be careful," she said. "Two of the three people he has killed were closely attached to his trial. His parole officer and the head attorney of the firm that worked to put him away. And I know there was some sort of skirmish between the two of you…"

"Yeah, there was. I lost the eye and these fingers," he said, holding up his right hand and revealing the stubs where his ring finger and pinky should have been. "But I'm a big boy. I'll be okay. And besides…he won't come for me. He kills me, he'll have the mob come down on him. I'm not associated with the mob anymore, but I still have friends on the inside. Ronald is smart. He knows better. Now, I ask again: how can I help you?"

"As a man who was once Biel's friend, do you know where he might have headed once he was released? Some sort of safe place that the authorities might not think to look?"

"Well, I think the mob connection is kaput. He burned that bridge to the ground. So outside of his old haunts, I really don't know. He had one friend that he hung with for a while. This was back when he was active in the mob, working as an enforcer. There was some stink over it because this friend was not in the mob. They might have been cousins or something. But honestly, I doubt he went there. I'm pretty sure there was some bad blood between them at the end. Rumor has it that this is the guy that might have put in that anonymous call that led to the feds finally catching Ronald."

There's someone that would for sure be on a revenge hit list, Avery thought.

"Do you know a name and address?"

"I do," he said. "The guy's name is Warren Reilly. He lives in one of those old rundown houses out on Florence Street, where that mill used to run on the end of the block. You know it?"

Avery nodded. She was in a rush, sure, but she felt that there was an opportunity here to delve a bit deeper—maybe to get a better understanding of Biel's true motives and skewed reasoning.

"Can I ask what the altercation between you and Biel was?" she asked.

Parrish lit up another cigarette, which he drew from a pack sitting by the ashtray. He seemed to consider things for a while—maybe whether or not he wanted to get into it at all. In the end, he nodded and took a drag of his smoke.

"Ronald was always an extremist. We knew it pretty quickly, but no one said much. He was violent and took things a little too far when he was sent in as an enforcer. He'd be sent in to break a finger or two just to get some information from a guy and end up breaking his hand, a few ribs, busting out a few teeth. You heard about the guy he nailed to the shed, right? Just before he was caught?"

"Yes. What about him?"

"He used to be friends with us, too. He was the biggest voice of reason, trying to keep Ronald under control. In the end, look at what happened to him. Anyway…all of this," he said, waving at his eyes and other hand, "happened about a month before he was caught. I was with him on a job and he went berserk. He was asked to scare the guy, maybe even break his leg if necessary. But Ronald lost it. The guy smarted off to him and Ronald killed him. He strangled him to death and while the guy was fighting to breathe, Ronald told him about how he was going to find the guy's wife and daughter and do all of this repugnant shit to them.

"So I sort of lost my temper. I threatened to report him, to see that he never worked with the mob again. We got into a fight. He pulled a knife and I had nothing—no knife, no gun. He cut off my fingers and stabbed me in the fucking eye. I think he would have killed me if he didn't think the rest of the mob would rain hellfire down on him. But really, I think that little temper tantrum was the beginning of the end for him—when things really started to unravel."

Avery could see from the almost blank expression in Parrish's eyes that he was not enjoying the process of dredging it all up. He took a long drag from his cigarette when he was done and looked at her through the smoke he blew out.

"You close to catching him?" he asked.

"I don't know," she said. "If Warren Reilly pans out as a reliable lead, then perhaps. Thank you for your time, Mr. Parrish."

She took a few steps back toward her car and then paused. She turned back to the stoop where Parrish was picking his book back up.

"One more question, Mr. Parrish. Do you by any chance know Howard Randall?"

Parrish thought about it for a moment and then shrugged. "It sounds familiar, but it's not anyone I know. Why?"

"Just asking," she said, and continued to her car.

As she pulled away, she tried to figure out how Howard would have known about Kevin Parrish. Had he been following Biel's case while he was behind bars? For that matter...

Did they know each other while in prison? They were *in the same building, after all. And they both had notorious reputations...*

She felt like this was a bit of a stretch, but it did answer a few questions if it was indeed true. And whether it was true or not, the weight of it was enough to push her on. She pressed her foot a little harder on the gas as she hit the street, placing a call to the A1 to get an address for Warren Reilly.

CHAPTER TWENTY FIVE

Ironically, Warren Reilly's house was located less than five miles away from the Weston Hotel. Parrish had been right to call it a rundown place. Most street kids referred to these types of houses as crack houses. It was low-income housing usually offered by defeated real estate agents to recently released convicts or former drug addicts looking to get back o their feet and reclaim their lives.

She found parking easily, as hardly anyone who lived on Florence Street and the surrounding blocks could afford their own transportation. She knocked on the door and waited for a while only to have no one answer. She leaned toward the door, listening for signs of life, but there were none. She knocked again and this time, after no one answered, she tried the knob. It turned freely in her hand.

She creaked it open just a bit and called inside. "Mr. Reilly? Warren Reilly? Are you here?"

The only response she got was her own voice bouncing from the dingy walls. From simply placing her head inside the partially opened door, she could tell that the house was humid. And there was also an intense garbage smell, like piles of it waiting in the kitchen to be carried off to the city dump.

"Mr. Reilly, if you're here, this is Detective Avery Black with the Boston PD. I'm coming in because the door was open and under suspicion of criminal activity."

It was all bullshit, but Reilly didn't need to know that. *If* he was here.

The house was a dingy mess. Wallpaper was peeling, the floorboards were filthy, and she spotted a cobweb in the entryway, complete with two plump flies ready to be feasted upon.

The small entryway led into a den area that also served as the living room. She had to go no farther than that.

Warren Reilly was sitting on the couch. Several other flies, these very much alive, were circling around his head. Some landed on it, crawled around, and took off again. Warren Reilly did not seem to mind. Even before she got to the front of the couch to verify, Avery was fairly certain he didn't notice due to the two gunshot wounds in his forehead. Then, as if for good measure, a serving fork had been shoved into his stomach. Blood from the fork wound had seeped over his bare belly and into the couch cushions.

The peculiar thing was that this blood was almost completely dried.

Biel visited him first, she thought. *When he decided to start his little plan, he came to Warren Reilly first. According to Parrish, the two were close and then came to a bad end. Looks like Warren Reilly came to the worst end, though...*

Avery ventured around the rest of the house while she called in the scene to A1. She found no other signs of foul play; there were no cute cryptic notes, no obvious signs of Biel damaging the house or Reilly's property. She *did* see that a few drawers in the kitchen were opened. The silverware drawer looked to have been rummaged through the most—presumably where the serving fork had come from.

She walked back into the living room, looked Reilly over again, and then stepped back outside.

This is getting out of hand, she thought.

She found that she wanted to be back at the hospital, sitting with Ramirez. Knowing that he was now able to speak to her and that there was a certain ring to be discussed made this nightmare of a case seem almost offensive.

She headed back down to her car to wait for the cavalry to arrive. While she waited, she called the hospital to get a report on Ramirez's condition. According to the night nurse on duty, everything looked good—no different than from when she had been there earlier, but even that was a good sign. She badly wanted to ask if they could connect her to his room but she decided not to. Best to let him rest. All he would do would be to ask her about her case anyway. And she didn't want him overworking his brain in his condition.

She killed the call and nearly called Rose to check in on her as well. But before she had the chance, the saw a series of red and blue lights coming up from behind her.

She stepped out of her car and waited for them to pull in behind her. She wasn't too surprised to see O'Malley stepping out of his car—not a patrol car but nice sleek black number he used when on duty. As he came over to her, two other officers and another A1 detective got out of their respective cars and headed over.

Avery was prepared to brief them before they entered but before they could reach her, O'Malley waved them away. "Your show, guys," he said. "Relay anything new to Finley."

"What?" Avery asked, confused.

CHAPTER TWENTY SIX

The world was a blur when Avery got to Tricia's residence. She lived in a small townhouse in a cute neighborhood not too far away from Jack's place. She had instructed him to move somewhere else for a while and Biel had still found him. When O'Malley pulled the patrol car up to the lot, there were already two patrol cars parked there, painting the townhouse in washes of red and blue strobing light.

O'Malley had barely stopped the car before she was reaching for the door handle.

"Avery, wait," he pleaded. "Let me come with you."

She didn't bother with a response. As she ran up the walk, her mind and heart seemed to be quarreling. On one side, she was having to accept that fact that although she had fallen far out of love with Jack many years ago, she had still spent almost ten years of her life with him. And on the other side…she tried to imagine breaking the news to Rose.

"Oh God," she said under her breath.

As she reached the stairs, she saw two policemen talking. They apparently recognized her, as they stepped aside without question. From behind her, she heard O'Malley rushing up the sidewalk, still calling her name.

She stopped running the moment she stepped into the place. It felt cold and she could smell blood. Images of what Mitch Brennan's house had looked like earlier that day flashed through her mind.

God, was that really today? The amount of death she'd seen today was too much…coupled with Jack having sex with his young girlfriend.

And now this…it was surreal.

But it became something much darker when she saw the first smear of blood. It was just a few drops at first, splattered on the carpet. A policeman stepped out from behind the open archway between the entry hallway and the kitchen. He looked alarmed at first, ready to scold whoever had crept into this crime scene, but then saw her face.

"Detective Black," he said. "Um…do you need a minute, or…?"

O'Malley entered the hallway from the front door behind her. He was flushed, a little out of breath, and doing his best to play a supportive role. "Yes, Officer," he said. "Give us a minute, would you?"

The officer nodded sadly and walked out behind them.

"Avery, are you sure you want to see this?"

He knows it's bad, she thought as she stepped into the kitchen. *He knows it's going to be bad and is trying to make sure I don't break from this.*

There was a large pool of blood on the kitchen floor. It was mostly wet, but dried at the edges. *This happened at least two hours ago,* she thought. *Maybe a little later than that. No more than four hours after I visited him, that's for sure.*

She stepped around the edge of the counter and saw Tricia. She was lying face down in the same pool of blood. The back of her head had been hit hard, her skull clearly caved in. The marble cutting board that had been used as a weapon lay broken in the floor next to her. But there was also a large butcher knife planted in the base of her spine. That, too, was bleeding but not as profusely as the massive wound on the back of her head.

She looked to the living room wall straight ahead of her. There was a message written in blood. The roll of paper towels used to write it had been left on the sofa.

EVERYONE YOU LOVE

That was all it said.

Avery felt a pure flash of hatred and anger sizzle for a moment but it quickly disintegrated into something that felt far too much like helplessness.

The kitchen gave way to the living room and before she even crossed into it, she saw the hand; it was barely uncovered by the base of the small kitchen bar. She trembled, her eyes never leaving it as she stepped into the living room.

She couldn't help it—she let out a sob and her knees almost gave out.

Jack was sprawled out on his back, his right leg bent awkwardly from the fall. His throat had been cut in the same way as Jane Seymour's but that was not the end of it. Not by a long shot.

There was so much blood. It was everywhere. Before she forced herself to tear her eyes away from Jack, she saw at least five more wounds. They all looked to be made by a knife, probably the same one that was sticking out of Tricia's back. Two in his chest, one in his groin, and one in the side of his face that had split open the corner of his mouth.

She turned around and blinked away the tears.

Rose, she thought. *My God...Rose.*

"Who discovered the bodies?" she asked, her voice thin and meek.

"The neighbor. Said he received a call from Jack, saying he needed help. But when the neighbor got here, she found this."

"Excuse me," a soft voice said from behind them. It was the officer who had stepped out not three minutes ago. "I thought you might want to know that the number on the neighbor's phone was Jack's. But the phone isn't here. We're trying to trace the location of the call right now. We're assuming the killer stole it, placed the call so the bodies would be discovered, and then ditched it."

She listened and understood what was being said, but none of it seemed to fit. She was still having trouble believing it was happening at all. All of that blood on the floor...it couldn't be real, could it? That wasn't really Jack, was it?

"Avery," O'Malley said. "Listen to me. He's getting careless. He stole a phone. He used a knife and a cutting block here. We'll get a print. We'll find the phone and get an idea of where he might have gone."

Rose...

That was the only thing going through her head in that moment. As she thought of her daughter, her concern became less and less about having to break the news of her father's death to her. The main concern was now for her safety.

Yes, she knew that there were two men stationed at the motel. Sawyer and Dennison. But Biel was crazy, desperate, and very motivated.

She looked back at the message on the living room wall, written in smears of maroon.

EVERYONE YOU LOVE

"Rose," she said.

"What?" O'Malley asked.

"I need to get back to Rose. Right now."

"Okay, yeah. Jesus... I have to stay here on the scene until forensics shows up. Take my car. I'll catch one of these guys back toward the A1. If you need anything at all, call Finley. Got it?"

She only nodded firmly as O'Malley offered her his keys and she snatched them from his hand.

"My God, Avery," he said. "I'm so sorry...Rose..."

She assumed he had just figured out what she was going to have to do when she got back to the motel—what she was going to have to tell her daughter.

Everyone you love. That message replayed over and over in her head like a taunt.

A taunt which she effectively quieted with her own: *Over my dead body.*

CHAPTER TWENTY SEVEN

It was 11:10 when Rose jerked awake. She didn't even remember falling asleep. She looked to the TV and saw a rerun of *The Big Bang Theory*. She'd fallen asleep during some lame house hunting show. She guessed that had been around ten or so.

Her mind was so muddied by these thoughts that it took her a few moments to latch onto what really mattered.

Something just woke me up. Not something loud, really. Something...weird. Now what the hell was it?

As she climbed out of grogginess and into a full panicked state of awareness, a few things occurred to her. First, her mom wasn't there. And being so late, that was either a good thing (as she potentially was on the trail of the killer) or a bad thing. Whatever the reason, it meant that she was all alone.

No, she thought. *Sawyer and Dennison are right outside. You're safe. You're—*

But then she heard something else. This time, she heard it clearly, free of the veil of sleep. It was a thumping noise and what sounded like a deep intake of breath.

Never one to hide under the covers, even when she was a little girl, Rose cautiously stepped out of bed. The room was illuminated only by the faint glow of lights from the parking lot outside, spilling through the closed blinds and across the floor in soft white streaks. She went to the window and just before she pried the blinds open with her fingers to see what was going on out there, she thought better of it. She thought of that dead cat tied to the brick, crashing through her mom's window. Someone was after them; it would be stupid to be so careless as to simply open the blinds.

She dropped down to her knees and just barely lifted up the bottom blind. She was still unable to see much of anything, so she scooted over to where she was kneeling directly under the center of the window. She lifted the bottom of the blinds up as quietly as she could. At first, all she saw was the glare of the soft light outside against the window. But then her eyes started to adjust to the dark and she was able to make out shapes.

She saw the police car, parked directly in front of the room. The driver's side door was open, the interior light shining. In the seat, one of the officers—Dennison, she thought—looked to be sleeping. It wasn't until she saw the limp way his head hung that she realized that he wasn't sleeping at all. He was dead.

Just as this sank in, she saw another shape. This one was much closer to her, just to her right and on the concrete walkway in front of the room. It was two men, wrestling against one another. The thumping noise Rose had heard was one of them being slammed against the side of the building. As they fought one another, Rose managed to get a good grasp on what was happening—and it terrified her.

One of the men was Officer Sawyer. The other was a man she had never seen before. He was mostly bald and his eyes looked like reptilian slits in the dark. He was clearly winning the battle and the reason why was obvious. There was something sticking out of the side of Sawyer's neck. Even in the darkness and shadows, Rose could see the glistening blood pouring out of him.

"Shit," Rose breathed.

In doing so, she dropped the blinds a little too quickly. They clattered against the windowsill.

Outside, the bald man turned in her direction. Still fighting with Sawyer, the bald man actually smiled at her—an evil grin she barely saw through the jostled blinds.

Rose went stumbling back so quickly that she struck the bed— the bed her mother should have been sleeping in, but where was she anyway? She hated that she felt nothing but anger toward her mother in that moment, but there it was. She scrambled to her feet, let her logic and instinct come to the forefront of her mind, and rushed for the door. It was already locked, but she also set the chain lock as well.

She then backed away from the door and went to the bedside table that sat between the two beds. She scooped up her phone and scrolled to her mother's number. With her thumb hovering over her mom's name, something slammed into the door from outside.

Rose jumped, let out a yelp, and her phone went flying out of her hand. It bounced almost effortlessly on the bed and as Rose dove for it, something slammed into the door again. She could hear the chain rattling, the lock trembling.

Rose shrieked and every nerve in her body kicked into fight-or-flight mode. The phone forgotten, all she could think about was trying to survive. She ran as fast as she could into the bathroom, nearly colliding with the sink. As she turned around to close the door behind her, the door to the room was struck again.

The top hinge popped out from the door frame and door shook loosely in its frame. Another hard attack and it would likely come falling down. Crying now, Rose slammed the bathroom door and set the lock. As her shaking fingers set it, she realized that the locking mechanism for the bathroom door was much weaker than the door to the room. Still, she felt as if she had made progress, that she had run away from the bald man and really, that was all she could do.

But now, trapped in the bathroom with no way out, it seemed like a stupid move. And with that move having pinned her here, she realized just how terrified she had been when she had dashed into the bathroom. She'd even left her damned phone out there on the bed. Not that it mattered…the guy would be in here any moment now and that would be the end of it. She might have enough time to place the call—might even get to hear a ring or two from her mom's phone—but that would be it.

As if to confirm this, she heard a loud crashing noise from the other side of the bathroom door. The man was inside. He'd managed to kick the door down.

Someone had to see him kill the cops, she thought. *And even if not, surely someone heard him kicking at the door. Where the hell is the manager?*

"Your mother isn't here?" the bald man said as he neared the bathroom door. She could hear his walking in her direction and then a sound like he was running his fingers down the door in an almost sensual manner. "Of course she isn't," he said, answering his own question. "She's out cleaning up my messes. And maybe…well, maybe she has some bad news for you. I almost want to tell you myself before I kill you. Do you want to know it?"

"Go to hell!" She screamed this at him, but did not feel defiant at all. Then, following this, she screamed as loud as she could, trying to attract as much attention as possible.

"Ah, bad girl," the man said. And with that, he started to kick at the bathroom door. The bottom of the door buckled easily, the old wooden frame splintering.

Rose looked around for anything she could defend herself with. But there was nothing. Not even a plunger.

I'm going to die, she thought. It was a horrifying thought but one that she nearly managed to accept with a shaky sort of clarity. She'd been hiding her fear to this point through pretending to be pissed at her mom—to shut her out and resort to the sad little teenage moods she'd used to her advantage a few years back. But really, she'd be scared, but didn't want her mom to know. Now she was staring that fear in the face and it was like finally meeting some dark stranger and accepting them for what they were.

The next time the door shook, it came crashing in. The man had thrown his shoulder into it and it had come down easy. Maybe a little *too* easy. The bald man had clearly not expected it to come down with such speed. He nearly fell down, and probably would have if he had not reached out and grabbed the sink with a flailing right hand.

As he balanced himself along the side of the sink, his eyes fell on Rose in an embarrassed sort of way, as if to say *I don't know my own strength.*

And it was that cocky look that bought Rose a single second. As he tried to quickly correct himself, his right foot got caught on the fallen door, wedging his shoe between the downed door and the floor.

Seeing this, Rose bolted for the door. He reached out for her, snatching at her. A blood-soaked right hand caught her shoulder and drew her back. But his grip was slick with the blood of the two cops he had just killed and Rose was able to pull away quickly.

She made it out of the bathroom and instantly went for her phone. She grabbed it and then headed straight for the door. She didn't dare look back over her shoulder. She kept her eyes on the opened door and the night beyond.

She was three steps away from it when she felt the full weight of the bald man fall on her back. He had apparently leaped at her, crashing into her back and sending her to the floor straight ahead and slightly to the left. Her right arm struck the edge of the bed frame and a shuddering pain like electricity raced through that entire side of her body.

He grabbed her by the hair and rolled her onto her back roughly. She tried to cry out but before she could, he punched her hard in the stomach. As she gasped for air, he caressed the side of her face. She felt that he was wearing gloves, even through the coating of blood.

"I'm going to kill you now," he said simply. "It'll be quick; I don't have time to show off. But first, let me tell you my secret. Do you know where I've come from? Do you know who I killed before I came to pay you a visit? Would you like to know?"

She whined through her gasps for breath. She heard his words but they seemed to float away into some other place. She wanted to close her eyes as he settled his full weight against her, wanted go deaf to stop hearing his voice.

Then his hands were on her throat, squeezing.

And then his mouth was at her ear, like some demented lover, about to tell her his secret.

* * *

Avery saw Sawyer's body before she was even across the parking lot. Seeing it, she brought her car to a screeching halt, one wheel coming up on the edge of the concrete walkway that ran along the length of the place, connecting the rooms. As she got out of the car, the engine still running and the headlights still on, she saw the patrol car. The door was opened. The interior light was on, glowing dimly down on Dennison.

She barely paid Sawyer any attention as she ran toward Rose's room. Even so, she still saw smears of blood on the concrete and against the side of the motel's exterior wall. She drew her gun and after that, her instincts all went into panicked-mother mode rather than trained detective.

"Rose?" she called out, even before entering the room. "Rose, baby…are you okay?"

She was nearly weeping with anticipation and gut-wrenching fear as she stepped into the room.

She had taken only one step before she saw something come swinging for her head. She stepped backward just in time and could feel whatever it was pass by the tip of her nose by no more than an inch. When it crashed into the door—which she now realized had been kicked in with force—she was vaguely aware that someone was swinging the base of a lamp at her.

She then saw the bald head and the leering face of Ronald Biel. There were flecks of blood on his face, stretching from his brow to the lopsided sneer he gave her as he dropped the lamp and came at her with his bare hands.

Avery brought her Glock up and fired just before his gloved hands touched her throat. The shot caught him high in the left shoulder, spinning him like a top. He slammed into the door frame and then stumbled out onto the concrete. Torn between her need to stop Biel and her heartbreaking need to find Rose, Avery missed a beat and glared around the room.

She found Rose, lying on the floor. There were bloody handprints around her neck. Her eyes were open, but she was not moving.

Avery's body went slack for a moment and she thought she might collapse to the floor. But then she felt the reassuring weight of the Glock in her hands. She let out a moan that tried to evolve into a scream as she turned back toward Biel.

He had made his way outside now, running as well as he could into the parking lot. He was about eight feet away, favoring the side she had just shot. Avery brought up her gun, her hands trembling and her eyes blurring with tears.

She fired and knew right away that her current state sent the shot wide right. She steadied herself and fired off tow more shots. One took him high in the same shoulder. The other, she wasn't sure.

But he kept moving.

Avery's legs gave out then, the grief pulling her legs out from under her. She kept the gun raised and in a blur of pain and sorrow and absolute hatred, fired off nine more rounds, pulling the trigger until she heard all clicks.

She kept squeezing the trigger with her right hand as she used her left to get to her feet, pulling herself up by the door handle.

"Mom?"

Gasping in a shocked breath, Avery turned and saw Rose sitting up. She was pushing herself up by her elbows and looked very much out of it.

Rose ran to her and gathered her up in her arms, dropping the expelled Glock. "Rose! Oh my God! Are you okay?"

She nodded. "My throat hurts. He strangled me for a while, I think. But then he heard your car pulling up. But…Sawyer and Dennison…"

"I know, honey," she said.

"Mom…he said he had a secret. That he had been somewhere before he came here. What was he talking about?"

Avery's heart felt like it was being wrung dry. "Hold on, baby," she said. "I have to call this in—"

"Mom? Please. Tell me."

Slowly, she took Rose's hand and told her. And although she did not think it possible, the night seemed to grow about ten shades darker.

CHAPTER TWENTY EIGHT

Weston Motel was a circus within twenty minutes. The entire parking lot was awash in headlights as patrol cars and sedans pulled into the lot. Avery and Rose remained in their room, which was getting quite crowded. Avery was relaying what had happened to Connelly while an EMT looked Rose over.

Rose had a few bruises on her neck but there seemed to be no real damage done. She had also been looked over to see if Biel might have left prints on her but because he had been wearing gloves, there was nothing. The same was true of Sawyer and Dennison. And although no one had been there to witness what had happened to them, the running theory was that Dennison's throat had been slit and then he had been stabbed in the chest and stomach a total of six times.

As for Sawyer, it was believed that he had stepped away for a moment to get a cup of coffee from the front desk, as there was a mostly empty paper cup near his body and the smell of coffee mingled with blood. He had been stabbed with the same knife used to kill Dennison. There had been only two wounds on Sawyer—one in his side that had likely punctured a lung, and then another in his throat, where the knife had remained lodged in. Rose had described seeing something sticking out of his upper chest area when he had been wrestling with Biel as she spied the match through the bottom of the blinds.

It was not a pretty picture, but it was the picture they had.

Through all of the commotion, Avery managed to ignore most of it and focus on Rose. She'd had only five minutes or so to grieve the loss of her father with just the two of them before the first cop car had arrived. Since then, she looked like a zombie, staring off into space. She'd answer questions when they were asked of her but that was about it. Avery wanted to yell at everyone in the room and those gathered outside to tell them to give them a chance to process it all. The girl had just lost her father for God's sake, could they get a little bit of privacy?

But when she saw the first news van pull up outside, she knew that any hope for privacy was gone.

Connelly was standing in front of Avery, clearly a little out of his element. Avery had never seen him at a loss before. It did not look good on him.

"You fired every single round," Connelly said. "And you say you're only sure you hit him twice."

"Yes," she said. "I'm sorry. But I thought Rose was dead and I lost my mind there for a moment."

"That's understandable," he said. "But you hit the bastard. Twice. So he's bleeding. And if he's bleeding, that means he probably left some sort of a trail. Which way was he heading?"

"I don't know. Just straight across the parking lot is all I know for sure."

"Okay. Let me get some guys on that. I'll be right back."

She watched Connelly walk through the door and then turned back to Rose. The EMT was finishing up, giving her a nod of approval.

"She's lucky," the EMT said. "No serious damage from what I can see. If she reports trouble breathing or any sort of pain in her neck in the next few days, you may want to get X-rays done. But I think she'll be fine."

From outside, she could hear people shouting. She went to the wrecked door and looked out. A line of four cops was trying to hold back a news crew. As she watched this, another news van pulled in. More headlights trailed behind that.

"What now, Mom?" Rose asked.

It was a good question. And she hated herself for not having any answers. She had run herself ragged today and had nothing to show for it other than two dead cops, a dead former co-worker, and a dead ex-husband.

He's calculating it all, she thought. *He's on a schedule. Nothing random. He's got some sort of order to it all, presumably with me at the end of it. He went for Rose after Jack. So would I be next? If so, why did he run so easily? Yes, I shot him but if he set this whole thing up for me, he wouldn't have just retreated like that, would he?*

That particular train of thought was trying to lead somewhere. Maybe if it wasn't so late and she weren't dealing with Jack's death, she could figure it out. She tried following it where it was leading her but before she could find where it ended, a large shape came marching across the parking lot.

Mayor Greenwald looked like some sort of elongated shadow as he neared her. It was clear that he was not used to being awake at this hour. He looked pissed—almost aghast at the situation before him. Avery almost wished the bodies of Sawyer and Dennison hadn't yet been covered up. She knew how Greenwald hated the sight of blood.

As Greenwald neared the room, Avery saw Connelly also running over. He could apparently see the tension between them, radiating like telekinetic energy in a superhero movie. He could sense an explosion on the way and was trying to stop it.

He was a few steps too short, though. Greenwald came up to the doorframe, his face red with pent-up rage. Avery stood her ground, though. She had never been intimidated by fabricated power and she sure as hell wasn't going to start now.

"And where the hell were you when this happened?" he asked, basically growling at her.

With just as much force, she responded, "I was at a crime scene where I found my ex-husband's body. So if you really want to get into this with me right now, you might want to rethink your approach."

He chuckled, but his eyes shot beyond her shoulder and to Rose, sitting on the bed and staring blankly at the wall. "You threatening me, Black?"

"If you're planning on getting in my way of finding this bastard, then yes. Consider it a threat."

"Wait, now," Connelly said, finally making it over. "The two of you need to take a moment to—"

"Did you put her on this case?" Greenwald asked, interrupting.

"Yes," Connelly said. "She's the best I have and I'd do it again. Now, however," he said, "Avery…after your ex-husband, I have to ask you to sit out. You're too close to it."

"I was too close to it after a cat came crashing through my window with a note attached to it," she said.

"I can't believe the gall of the two of you," Greenwald said. "When this is over, I'll see to it that heads will roll through the A1. I'll have you know that I—"

"You'll do *nothing*," Avery said. "Because you want Biel caught as badly as I do. You have votes to consider, after all." With each word, her voice grew louder and louder until she was shouting into his face. "You have two cops dead, and that makes *at least* six people this asshole has killed in *one day*! So if you want it to stop, you'll keep your nose out of business it knows nothing about and stay the fuck out of my way."

"You can't—"

"Captain," she said, ignoring Greenwald and looking straight at Connelly. "Could you please remove the mayor from my doorway

132

so I can close it and be alone with my daughter during this difficult time?"

Without waiting for an answer, she reached out for the broken door and forced it closed as Greenwald stood there, forced to take a step backward. The door would not close all of the way because of Biel's attack, but she got her point across.

She looked to Rose and saw that even though there were tears coming down her cheeks, she was grinning. "You can be a bad ass when you want to be," Rose said. "Have you always been this cool?"

"No."

She sat down beside Rose and took her in her arms. As Rose wept openly against her, Avery let her own tears out. She had never been so conflicted. Should she stay with Rose and be the supportive mother in her time of need or should she head back out to look for Biel?

The more she thought about the decision she needed to make, the more she started to lose it. She and Rose wept together and through her tears, Avery said something that seemed to come out of her mouth with ease.

"This is my fault," she said. "Rose...the things I've done in the past. I'm sorry. I threw Biel's case. He's coming after me and because of that you're at risk. Because of that your father is dead and—"

She stopped there, feeling a torrent of sorrow coming on that she feared she would not be able to stop.

"No way, Mom. You didn't make this guy nuts. You weren't part of the system that allowed him to get out on good behavior."

"But I *am* the one that sent him to jail. The evidence was flimsy and I...I should have done my job. But he's sick, Rose. The man is sick and I had to make sure he went to prison. I don't know which job made me lose more of my soul—defending people like Biel or chasing them down with a badge and a gun. Kiddo...I'm so sorry."

She didn't know how long they sat there together. At some point, Rose fell asleep against her shoulder. Avery gently laid her back, her head on the pillow, and quietly got out of the bed. She checked the bedside clock, saw that it was 1:36, and went to the door. She opened it and peered outside. The news crews were still there; she counted at least four of them now.

But she also saw six police cars and two black cruisers. In the crowd of police, she spotted O'Malley. He was speaking to Connelly beside a patrol car. Finley was also in the crowd, speaking to someone on his cell phone.

Checking back on Rose one last time, Avery stepped outside. The night was cold, but that was good. It kept her awake and alert. She walked directly over to Connelly and he gave her a grave expression.

"That was some shit you pulled on Greenwald," he said. "If I don't fire you in the next week or so…"

"We'll worry about that later," she said. "What can I do?"

"Nothing," Connelly said. "Spend time with your daughter."

"She's asleep and there are easily fifteen cops here right now. She's safe. So I ask you again, what can I do?"

"Look," O'Malley said. "We've got every available man looking for Biel right now. They've even started reporting it on the news—for citizens to be on the lookout for him. They've put up his picture and everything. Six murders in a little more than a single day. Boston is a city that takes care of itself. With the public in on this, we'll find him."

Avery found herself wishing Ramirez were there with her. She was so unsure of what to do with herself, and Ramirez had always grounded her. She was at her best when he was at her side. She thought with precision and was always sharp and on point, With Ramirez, she…

Ramirez.

Her thoughts came to a halt as she looked back to O'Malley. "You said you have *every* man on this?"

"Yes. This fucker is going to meet his end sooner rather than later."

She almost voiced her concern out loud but kept it to herself. *What about the guard outside of Ramirez's hospital room?* she wondered. *Was he called away, too?*

If she raised this concern, there would be too much time wasted with Connelly telling her not to worry about it and sending someone over to stand guard. And she was sensing that time was not something she had very much of. With Jack dead and an attempt made on Rose's life, there was only one other person Biel might go after that she cared about.

No…he can't. Not in a hospital.

But she then thought of Sawyer and Dennison, watching over Rose. Trained policemen, now dead.

"Can I get a ride to the hospital, then?" she asked. "I hate to ask but I don't trust myself to drive. I need to see Ramirez. Please."

"Sure," Connelly said. "As long as you stay away from this. We have this covered, Black."

134

"I know," she said. "And can you please just make sure Rose is taken care of?"

"I'll stay here myself until you get back," O'Malley said. "Me and at least four others."

"Thank you."

"In the meantime," Connelly said, "tell Finley to give you a ride. It might help him. He and Dennison were pretty good friends."

With a nod of appreciation, Avery did just that. She found Finley's face in the crowd and walked over to him quickly. Her watch read 1:43 now and she could sense something very close to finality in the air. The morning was on the way but she had a feeling that by the time the sun broke the horizon, this would be over.

For her, or for Biel—that was the question.

CHAPTER TWENTY NINE

Finley *did* seem glad to leave the scene at the motel but as he drove Avery to the hospital, he said very little. The night had taken its toll on most of the officers in the A1 as news of Sawyer and Dennison had made the rounds. She could also tell that he was very uneasy about being with her and not knowing what to say about Jack's death. Finley was a real sweetheart but he was not so good with consoling.

As they came to the parking garage, Avery realized that somewhere between screaming at Mayor Greenwald and getting in the car with Finley, a spike of adrenaline had coursed through her. She was wired and jittery, leaning forward in her seat as Finley flashed his card to the guard in the little parking shack.

As he made his way to the first available spot, Avery heard his phone ringing. He answered it right away, ever diligent and eager to please. Avery only halfway listened in to the conversation as he parked the car.

"This is Finley."

There was a heavy silence in the car after this. Avery looked to Finley and saw a momentary flinch to his expression. He had just gotten some news that had rocked him and he was trying to hide it.

"Who is it?" Avery asked.

Finley rubbed at his forehead and shook his head. "Shit," he said.

"Finley…what is it?"

He looked to her, the phone still to his ear. His eyes were wide and she could see tears glistening in them.

Avery said nothing at all and moved quickly. She opened the door and the moment her feet hit the pavement, she was running. A few seconds later, he heard Finley's voice calling after her.

"Avery! No. Wait!"

But she was already out of the parking garage and running across the thin strip of road that led to the hospital. The look she had seen in Finley's eyes remained fixed in her mind's eye and she prayed that she wasn't just jumping to conclusions. But when she came to the sliding doors and opened to the primary waiting room, she saw five members of the hospital staff and security huddled behind the desk. One of them looked up and saw her. As they were about to say something to her, she held up her badge and kept running.

She didn't bother with the elevators, opting for the stairs instead. She took them two by two all the way to the fourth floor. She basically slammed into the door that opened up to the hallway.

Her cell phone rang in her pocket but she ignored it. Ahead of her, almost all the way down the hall in the direction of Ramirez's room, several people were milling around. Some were doctors but at least two were hospital security.

"No," she breathed.

But the distant wail of police sirens in the faraway distance told her everything she needed to know.

She barreled down the hall. She ran fast and with hitching breaths. As she neared the crowd at the end of the hallway, she didn't even bother with her badge anymore. When the first guard tried stopping her, she shoulder checked him, sending him toppling backward into a nurse. The commotion caused just enough of a distraction for her to make it into Ramirez's room.

She pushed through the door and stepped inside.

She nearly tripped over the body of a man in a black shirt and pants, similar to what hospital security was wearing. When she halted and nearly stumbled over him, she looked to the bed.

Ramirez was there, lying in bed. His head was tilted slightly to the right, peering in her direction as if he had been waiting for her. His eyes were open and that, to Avery, was the most heartbreaking part.

Because it was clear that he was dead.

Her knees buckled as she walked toward him and when she hit the bedside and took his hand, she screamed into the mattress, so hard that her lungs hurt, so hard that for a moment, she lost herself in it and she was dead, too.

***

She knew a few things for certain and managed to patch them together about half an hour later.

In the midst of her screaming, another security guard had come into the room and dragged her out with the help of another doctor. She was then escorted into another room where she continued to scream and cry. Her throat went hoarse and she was given water. At some point, Finley showed up and his face was the only real beacon of hope in the place. He tried to hug her but she wouldn't let him.

137

She sat in a chair and rocked back and forth. Finley came in and out of the room. After a while, Connelly was also there. He kept going in and out of the room. At some point, he brought her coffee. She drank it slowly as she kept seeing Ramirez's dead eyes staring at her.

Time slipped by. She wasn't sure how much time had passed when her mind seemed to tether back to reality. It could have been five minutes, it could have been a day. When she did finally feel her mind come back to its former self, Connelly was in the room with her. Just the two of them. He was simply staring at her, holding his own cup of coffee in his hands.

"How?" was all she asked.

"There are parts that are still uncertain and it's an utter embarrassment on this hospital's part," Connelly said. "But here's what we know for certain. "At exactly one fifteen, a man came into the emergency room with two gunshot wounds to his upper torso. The name he gave—get this—was Ronald Randall. He waited about three minutes before a doctor saw him. That doctor was found dead around one forty-five. At exactly one forty-seven, a nurse went into Ramirez's room just to check up on him. She found the hospital guard that had been placed outside of his room dead on the floor, a scalpel in his throat. Shortly after that, it was discovered that Ramirez was dead."

"How?" she asked again.

"Avery…what's it matter?"

"How?"

"Suffocation," Connelly said. "Pretty sure it was a pillow over his face. "We've got the staff checking over footage of the hospital from the time span between one fifteen and two o'clock for any sign of Biel. He can be seen in one shot, heading for the elevators on this floor, and then again, thirty seconds later, walking right out of the emergency room doors. That was at one fifty—exactly an hour and a half ago."

"No one has found him?" she asked.

"Not yet. And look. There's one more thing. And I need you to listen to me. You are not to go back into his room. You try it, and I *will* arrest you. But…this was found on the wall."

He handed her his phone, with a picture pulled up on it. She studied it and found another message from Biel. This one was written in Sharpie, in his unmistakable handwriting.

Two words. That was all. And it was like he was starting to taunt her all over again.

Just sittin', the message read.

She handed it back to him as her heart flared with rage.

"That mean anything to you?" Connelly asked.

In her head, she could picture Biel sitting in the visitation room just before the trial. He'd hated silence and would often fill it with whistling softly. And of course, as it had over the last day or so, it came down to that whistling solo from Otis Redding's "Sitting on the Dock of the Bay."

She heard it in her head in that moment. Too clear, as if the bastard was in the room with her. She recalled some of the lyrics and again, a surge of anger roared through her.

Just sittin' on the dock of the bay.

Just sittin'.

"Avery? Anything? Does it mean anything to you?"

"No," she lied.

"Avery…what can I do for you right now? Is there anything at all?"

"I need to get back to Rose," she said.

"OK. I'll have Finley take you and—"

"No. Just…I need to be alone. Please."

"Of course," Connelly said. "Whatever you need."

Avery got to her feet. Her blood was boiling. She could feel tension forming in her shoulders and even in the way her jaw was set. She tried her best to seem defeated and relaxed, almost lethargic as she stood in front of Connelly.

"We'll get him," Connelly said. "By the time you wake up in the morning, Biel will be in custody. There's no way he's getting away this time."

"I know," she said. "Thanks, Connelly."

"Sure. Go get some sleep."

"I plan on it," she said.

Of course, that was another lie. Because as she left the room and headed down the hallway like a ghost not sure where to haunt, the little whistling tune from "Sitting on the Dock of the Bay" whispered through her head in a broken loop.

And she was suddenly sure of where this was all going to end.

CHAPTER THIRTY

First, she went back to the Weston Motel. It was 3:45 when she arrived. Even before she was able to make it to her parking spot, she saw a flurry of activity among the two police cars that were parked in front of her room. O'Malley came rushing over to her right away as she stepped out of her car.

And he kept coming. He came in close and did something so unexpected that Avery nearly fell down on the pavement.

He hugged her.

"Avery, I'm so sorry about Ramirez."

She hugged him back because it seemed like it was the right thing to do. She was pretty sure he was weeping, but she did her best to ignore it. She knew she had some genuine sadness lurking within her and when the time was right, she'd let it have its moment. But right now, everything felt almost mechanical within her. There was no time for sadness or grieving right now. Currently, she had only two things on her mind.

"I came to see Rose," she said.

"Yeah," O'Malley said, breaking the hug and trying to maintain some composure. "She's sleeping. But she asked about you. I had to make a decision…I told her about Ramirez. I hope that was okay?"

"That's fine," she said. "Thanks."

"We got her another room, too. With a lock and unbroken door and everything." He handed her a room key. *A17* sat in the center of its keychain.

She walked to the room and entered quietly, closing the door behind her so slowly that it didn't make any sound when it fit back into the frame. The room was another two-bed set-up, and Rose had taken the bed closest to the wall. Avery went to her and sat on the edge of the bed. Rose was indeed sleeping, but not very deeply.

Avery stroked her daughter's dark hair. Again, she felt the sadness wanting to well up but she choked it back down. She kissed Rose on the forehead and whispered, "I love you, kid. I'll be right back."

With that, she stood up and looked down at her daughter. She was overcome with an abundance of love—a love she had not felt in looking down on her daughter since the days she had slept in a crib. Rose was going to have to live the rest of her life without a father. And Avery would always feel partly to blame for that.

She bit at her bottom lip, causing the slightest bit of pain.

No tears, she thought. *Not yet.*

She turned and went back for the door. As her hand reached out for it, she heard Rose stirring in the bed behind her. And then, her voice: "Hey, Mom?"

"Yeah?"

"Sorry about Ramirez."

"Me, too."

"You okay?"

"I will be…maybe. Eventually."

Rose made a *hmmm* sound in the darkness. "You know where he is now, don't you? You're going after him?"

"I have to, baby. I'm sorry."

"Don't be sorry, Mom. Go find him and feed him his fucking heart. Just…come back to me, okay?"

"I will."

"I love you, Mom."

"And I love you."

With that, she made her exit. She had to, or else she was going to become a blubbering mess and the plans she had for the next few hours would be shot. She relocked the door as she stepped back out into the night—which was quickly winding down to morning.

Avery found O'Malley in the gathering of five policemen standing outside of their cars in the chilly night air. She waved him over as she walked back toward her car. He came quickly, having apparently sensed the urgency and resoluteness in her when he had hugged her a few minutes ago.

"I need you to do a few things for me, O'Malley," she said.

"Anything within my power, I'll get it done."

"Three things. First…if I'm not here when Rose wakes up, please make sure she eats something. Second, I'm going to get in my car and leave here when you and I are done talking. I don't want you to follow me and I don't want any questions asked."

"Avery, I can't do that. You know that…"

"Third," she said. "I'm going to text you soon. Maybe half an hour, maybe an hour. I don't know, exactly. It'll tell you where I am. And I want you there first."

"Avery, what are you—"

"I said no questions," she said. "Please, O'Malley. Do this for me. And when you get my text and leave here, I'm trusting you to leave Rose in the best care possible."

She knew she was sounding bossy, like some traumatized diva. But she didn't care. She knew what was riding on the next few hours and, quite frankly, the way she was perceived by others in the A1 wasn't high on her list of things to care about at the moment.

"Please," she added.

"Fine," he said. "But you said you'd text no later than one hour from now. Once one hour and five minutes goes by, I'm calling it in. I'll report you as missing if I have to."

"Fair enough," she said.

She walked quickly back to her car before O'Malley could say anything else. As she put on her headlights and backed out, she watched his figure shrink and then disappear altogether. She turned back out onto the streets and headed east, pretty sure it would be the last place this case would take her.

CHAPTER THIRTY ONE

At night, most of the docks along the Port of Boston looked almost majestic. Cargo ships came and went and, much further down the port along the downtown stretch, cruise ships would dock in from time to time. From the air, it all looked clean and promising, just another scenic area of Boston.

But as a detective, Avery knew better. She knew that there were nooks and crannies along the docks that were unsavory. In the shadows of the cargo ships and fishing hauls there were other activities usually taking place; these were activities that involved the trading of money for bodies or drugs or both. And it was all hidden in plain sight while business was being conducted as usual in waters and on piers and docks several hundred yards away.

Avery drove beyond Union Wharf, heading further south, where the docks got a little less typical, a little less safe.

She remembered the place well. Just off of the lesser known Newman's Wharf, down a side street that made it look as if you were about to run directly into the water but too a sharp turn down a hill to an old loading area for smaller vessels.

She'd been there before, of course. She'd been an attorney then, escorted by a policeman. The site of Biel's first victim's murder (outside of the mob executions, including one man nailed to the side of a shed). It had been the one scene Biel had physically been spotted at but still, there had never been any evidence.

On her first visit, it had been just after lunch time. It had been overcast but humid, just as summer had kicked spring to the side. But now it was pitch black and cold as she watched Newsman's Wharf pass by on her right. There was on boat anchored alongside it, but there were no lights shining from the boat. The only light came from two lone poles along the sides of the wharf, barely cracking the night on the dock or the water a few feet beneath it.

Up ahead, the road veered to the left and then came to the winding turn. The road branched off here; she could go straight and head downtown or she could take the curb and go down the hill, to the old loading area that sat like some forgotten doorway to another world. She chose the curb, winding slowly downward onto a route that sat beneath a thin two-lane bridge that ran between an old building that had once been a paper mill and the small roadway toward Newman's Wharf.

As she passed under the small bridge, she saw the empty area beneath it. To the right, there was a brick wall that she supposed had once served as a sublevel to the old forgotten building that had once been a paper mill. To the left, there was a dirt hill that led up to the road, with old concrete platforms that had once held pillars when the little bridge had been bigger up until the late '70s and some of the port had looked different.

And ahead of her, a concrete platform and the open water.

While she was a little uncertain as she parked the car, she was not the same scared woman she had been when she had come here as an attorney. She had some experience under her belt now. Not to mention her reloaded Glock and a hatred that was even now continuing to evolve into something that, quite frankly, was beginning to alarm her.

In her head, she could her Biel whistling that tune. And she could see the writing on the wall from Ramirez's room.

Just sittin'...

She reached for her door handle but hesitated. First, she grabbed her phone and pulled up a text screen. She entered O'Malley's name and typed in: **Under Newman's Wharf, by old paper mill.**

But she did not press Send. Not yet...

She pocketed her phone and opened the door. She left the car running, the headlights set to dim and pointed toward the bottom of the old loading platform. She stepped out onto the concrete, pulled out her sidearm, and walked down near the water.

The smell of the place was disgusting, a mix of garbage, fish, and neglect. The sound of the water pushing gently against the edge of the fractured end of the platform was almost hypnotic, like something on one of those help-you-sleep recordings.

As far as she could tell, there was no one else there. She could hear distant voices coming across the water, workers on wharfs and docks further down the port. But they may as well have been on another world because here, in this forgotten area, she felt stranded.

Maybe I got it wrong, she thought. *Maybe I got the message wrong. I'm so screwed up right now, I could be jumping at anything...any reason to think I'm closing in on him.*

Slowly, she walked down toward the water. She scanned left and right, looking for any shadow that seemed out of place. As she did so, her instincts started to take over, finely tuned mannerisms that had become a part of her over her years as a detective. She felt someone watching her, someone lurking somewhere in the shadows.

To her left, there was an ancient-looking stack of pallets, the boards gray with age and moisture from the water. Back on the other side, toward the brick wall of the paper mill, she heard a faint clicking noise. She strafed over in that direction and saw an old shuttered doorway that had been concealed in the shadows. One of the boards was loose, its nail scraping slightly against the side of the old door frame from the slight breeze.

If it's moving in the breeze, its been broken recently, she thought. *If it was like the other boards shuttering it up, old and derelict, that broken piece would have fallen out by now.*

She walked toward the doorway. It was thin and shrouded in darkness beyond the boards that blocked passage into the building. There was no question as to whether or not Biel was in there; she was sure that he was. The question was whether or not she called out to him, to let him know that she was here and ready to face him.

She gripped her gun tightly as she stepped closer. The doorway was ten feet away, then five—

She paused, hearing something behind her.

Footsteps. Coming quickly.

She wheeled around, bringing the gun up.

She never even got a chance to fire. By the time she realized that there was a fragment of one of those broken pallets coming at her, she didn't have time to throw up any defense. A section of pallet slammed into the side of her face. As she spun around and went to the ground, she did an instant body-check.

The boards are old and mildewed—much softer than they would have been when they were first constructed. Also, my left shoulder took the brunt of the force. I'm okay...I'm okay.

She tasted blood in her mouth as she rolled over and leveled her gun. She saw the shape of a man, still holding the pallet. Biel. He was bringing the pallet down again. She could hear the wood creaking in his hands.

She pulled the trigger just as the pallet slammed into her arms. The shot went directly into the ground. There was a muffled ricochet as she lost the grip on the Glock. A shock of sharp pain went rocketing through her arms. She heard a cracking noise and, for a moment, feared that one of her wrists had been snapped. But then she felt the wood fragments against her face and realized that the pallet had broken in half as it struck her arms and the ground.

She did her best to get to her feet as quickly as she could but the electric pain made it next to impossible to move her left arm.

The best she could do was pushed herself partially up and away, trying to retreat.

That turned out to be a mistake. It gave Biel access to her stomach, which he firmly sent a vicious kick into. A blast of pain soared through her stomach and into her chest. She came off of the ground and landed on her side.

She looked up at Biel as he came down to his knees. He straddled her, one knee on either side of her hips. Slowly, almost erotically, he reached to the waist of his pants where she saw a hunting knife had been sheathed into a small holster. He drew the knife out and looked at it lovingly.

Then, in a move so quick she barely saw it, he made a slicing gesture. She felt the blade slide easily through the skin of her cheek. It was a shallow cut; he was just playing with her. And the look in his eyes was one of pure madness. He planned on having fun with her before he inflicted any real pain.

She tried to fight back but was still gasping for breath. She had no idea where her gun was and although the pain in her left arm had now downgraded to pins and needles, she still couldn't manage to use it as well as she would have liked to.

"My God," Biel said, lowering his face to hers. The pressure against her stomach was immense, making it harder for her to gather her breath back. "I've been thinking about being back in your presence for all this years. Not just to kill you—although, that's coming very soon—but to appreciate you. All of you. Do you know that feeling?"

She nodded, hoping to lure him in. Playing into his psychosis might be the only way she could make it out of this. "I have," she gasped, still finding it hard to breathe.

This seemed to take him aback. "Oh, you *think* you have," he said. "But you don't know the—"

She took that moment to spit in his face. It was thick and blood-tinged and she had just enough force behind it to make sure it landed directly in his face.

His moment of utter surprise was only momentary. And she did everything she could to act on it. Utilizing a move she had only ever put to use during her Krav Maga classes at the gym, she pivoted her chest forward a bit and then brought her legs up fast and hard. The motion caused Biel to rock back just a bit...but just enough for Avery to wrap the bottoms of her legs around his neck.

With a cry of pain and determination, Avery turned onto her side as Biel fell to the ground, still locked between her legs. She could instantly feel him favoring his left side as he tried to escape, presumably from the gunshots he had taken earlier in the night. And still, without the full strength of her left arm and still not able to draw a full breath, she knew he'd escape from the move in no time at all.

She made a careful fist of her right hand and sat up. The muscles in her stomach ached from the motion but she endured it for as long as she could. As Biel managed to free his head bit by bit, Avery threw a series of hard punches into his head. One caught him on the side of the face, splitting open his eyebrow. One caught him in the side of the jaw, making a delicate sound as his teeth clicked together. She managed to land four punches before he wriggled out of the move. He scrambled to his feet but just as he made it, Avery braced herself on her elbows and sent a wide-arcing sweep to the left.

It worked, taking Biel's legs out from under him, but his legs were damned strong and a shock of pain slammed through her ankles with the impact. She heard the clatter of his knife striking the ground and falling out of his grip.

Gun. Knife. All somewhere here in the darkness, she thought.

However, as she got to her feet as quickly as she could, she reached for her cell phone instead. She pulled up the text she had composed for O'Malley and hit Send.

In front of her, Biel was getting to his feet. With rage and frustration coming to the surface like lava, Avery charged at him and threw a knee into his face. A hollow thud filled the empty concrete platform as her knee struck him directly in the skull. He went down with a shout but as he fell, he managed to grab her leg.

She went down with him, throwing her arms up to keep her face from smashing into the concrete. As she did, her forearm fell on something hard.

The handle of his hunting knife. She quickly pulled it to her, keeping it hidden.

"Jack," she gasped, trying to wrestle away from him, hoping the mere act of speaking might distract him. "Why'd you kill him?"

"He was your husband when you sent me to prison," Biel hissed as he twisted at her leg. "I imagined him sleeping with you constantly. It was not fair. You were working to keep me free but fucking him…it made you impure. Distracted you. It's one of the reasons you failed to keep me out of prison."

He was getting to his feet, still wrenching her leg. He was working to roll her onto her chest. She knew what he was trying to do—to expose the back of her knee and then stomp down, probably dislocating it or tearing something.

147

"Got a secret for you," she said as she fought against it. "I gave up that case. I wanted you in prison. I could have done so much better."

Again, she used his shocked reaction to her advantage. She brought the knife up and, in another sit-up position, brought it hard across his right wrist. She was pretty sure the cut went deep. There was enough resistance for her to have to put a little extra force behind her movement.

Biel screamed out and dropped her leg. He held his right wrist and she saw the blood flowing right away, even in the darkness.

Not wanting to waste a single moment, she adjusted her grip on the knife and lunged forward, going for his stomach. He managed to sidestep it and when he did, he brought his left hand down hard. She knew from having worked with him in the past that he was right-handed but his left hand still packed a wallop. It struck her on the same side of the face the pallet had landed and for a moment, she saw stars as she went to the concrete.

No more trying to distract him or shock him, she thought. *This is going to go to the death. It just has to be a fight. No mind games, no clever tactics.*

Yet as she told herself this, Biel was already running at her. She had just enough time to block the first kick with her forearm, but the one that came immediately afterward struck her in the stomach. Then a second time. Then a third, this one perfectly aimed at her ribs.

The pain in her right side was immense as a rib cracked. She felt it, sharp and debilitating for a moment.

But she then remembered that she still held the knife. He drew back for a fourth kick and instead of blocking it, she met his leg with her right hand. The knife sank into his ankle. She could feel the blade passing by bone in a grinding sensation along the handle.

Biel howled in pain and hobbled backward. Avery was only barely aware of this, though. The cut he had placed on her cheek was bleeding, running down her face and neck. She was pretty sure her face was already bruising from the pallet and his punches, and the pain in her ribs and stomach was among the worst pain she'd ever experienced.

Think of what he did to Ramirez, she thought. *Think of what he tried to do to Rose...*

She pushed herself to her knees with a cry of pain. She was dizzy and reeling but she had no problem focusing on Biel's figure, a few feet in front of her. He was leaning against the brick wall and although she could clearly see what he was doing, she couldn't believe it.

He was taking the knife out of his ankle. He screamed as he did it, through gritted teeth. His face was also bleeding, mostly from the opened eyebrow she had delivered through her punches.

He's not going to stop until one of us is dead, she thought.

She glanced around and still did not see the gun. What she did know, however, was that in about three seconds, he was going to have the knife again. And she couldn't afford for that to happen.

Still fighting to gather a full breath and leaning to the left to alleviate pain in her right side where the rib was broken, Avery stumbled to the pile of pallets. She saw that several were splintered and broken along the back of the pile. She picked up a section that was two boards wide and even though it was basically falling apart in her hands, she had felt less than five minutes ago just how much of an impact they still possessed.

Biel slid the last little bit of the blade out of his ankle and the moment it was free, Avery was there. She drew the section of pallet back like a baseball bat and swung for the fences. She struck him in the left side of the face as hard as her body would allow. Her ribs screamed bloody murder at the force of it yet she managed to draw back once more.

The first hit had dizzied Biel; he staggered against the wall like a boxer looking for a corner to rest in. By the time his head had cleared, Avery delivered another blow. This one took him right in the chest and doubled him over. With his back exposed, Avery raised the boards a third time and brought them down on the back of his head.

He went down hard and with a gasping sound of pain. But Avery did not stop.

"Jack and Ramirez," she said, feeling the sadness trying to escape but keeping it at bay with blow after blow. One to his back, one to his legs, and another to his head.

He let out a shaky breath that released a spray of saliva and blood from his mouth.

I could kill him right now, she thought. *A few more whacks to the head. Or just find my gun...I could do it. It would be easy.*

Or...he could spend the rest of his life in jail. That would be justice. What you want to do is murder.

She started to cry then when she realized she did not care. She was going to kill him. She would face the repercussions later. To hell with it.

With a flashing image of Ramirez's dead eyes in her head, she raised the boards again.

Just before it was overhead, Biel quickly tilted to the side and reached out toward her. Only *reach* was not what he was doing. He was *stabbing*.

A shard of the broken pallet she had been beating him with pierced the meat of her calf. The wood went directly into her skin and she could feel it as Biel pulled down on it.

She dropped the pallet and stumbled backward. When she fell hard on her backside, she immediately tried to grab the wood that he had stabbed her with but could not angle herself to do so. Somehow, in front of her, Biel was getting to his feet. He staggered back and forth as if drunk. His face was a bloody mess and even as he stumbled forward, he spit out a tooth and a lot of blood.

And he chuckled about it.

Avery tried to get to her feet. But a momentarily paralyzed left leg and a broken rib along her right side made that very difficult to do.

Biel brought a hard open-handed slap cross her face. And then another.

"Bitch," he said. "You're going to wish you hadn't told me your little secret. Now that I *know* you threw my case…I'm going to kill you. And then I'm going to get to your daughter. And for your sake and hers…let's just hope she's not a virgin…"

"No!" Avery screamed.

The next time Biel brought his hand across her face, it was in the shape of a fist.

Avery felt her jaw snap. She thought he might have broken it. But she found it hard to care as black dots started to infiltrate her vision. She was dimly aware that he was grabbing her by the collar of her shirt. The world came and went in fuzzy flashes as she fought against blacking out.

In the back of her head, she wondered how long it had been since she sent that text to O'Malley.

She then realized that Biel was dragging her forward. It was slow going because of his ankle. He fell down once, nearly on top of her. He chuckled maniacally the entire time. Blackness started to cloud her vision and she could feel herself going under.

No…fight it. Rose…she's depending on you. And Ramirez…his memory deserves better than this.

But it was too hard to fight. The pain was everywhere and it was just so much easier to give up. She closed her eyes, trying to focus and fight it off.

CHAPTER THIRTY TWO

Something ice cold forced her to open her eyes.

Her entire body seemed to be in a state of shock. She opened her mouth to gasp but couldn't. Something was in the way. Something cold. Something wet.

What the hell?

And then she felt her head being pulled upward. It hurt her neck but she was finally able to gasp—to breathe. And Biel was there, his voice in her ear and his bloodied face nuzzling next to hers.

"I hear the sirens," he said. "I suppose you had backup planned this whole time. But it doesn't matter. You're going to die, Avery."

She drew in a shaky breath but it was cut short as he pushed her head down again. And this time, she pieced together what was going on. His final punch had caused her to black out. But now he was going to drown her. Slowly. And the cold water had brought her back around. With her head pushed under the water, she did everything she could to not panic. Instead, she put together the fragments of her current situation.

They were at the broken lip of the old loading platform. Biel was kneeling at the edge of it. She was lying on her chest and he was pushing her head under. She was already short of breath and could feel her lungs desperately trying to find air.

Hopefully he'll want to taunt me some more, she thought. *Because if he doesn't pull my head up one more time, I'm going to drown.*

Her lungs were aching. It was almost as bad as the pain in her calf and ribs. She knew that soon, her body would start to spasm. Maybe that's what he was waiting for. If he heard the sirens of backup on the way, maybe he wouldn't be so slow about it after all.

But mercifully, he simply couldn't resist himself. She felt her head being pulled back up. She retched and coughed and drew in air greedily. Beside her, Biel was laughing.

"Is that bullshit about your life flashing before your eyes true?" he asked. His voice was garbled and wet. She thought there might be blood trickling down his throat.

Good, she thought. *Let him drown in it.*

Biel then planted a kiss on her cheek. It was sticky with blood. "It's been fun, Avery. Just know that when the police do show up, I intend to escape through that door I fooled you with earlier. I'll do everything I can to escape…and at some point, all of the things I dreamed of doing to you while I was in prison,…your daughter will be the lucky recipient of it all. I'll tell her you said it was okay."

She tried to fight against him but he had a knee of her back now, pinning her to the concrete.

She felt his hands in her hair and then he started pushing down. "Biel—"

Avery barely heard the voice and for a moment, thought it was her own—pleading with him, maybe. But no…it was another voice. A man's…coming from the darkness behind them.

Biel turned around and when he did, he released Avery's head. Whimpering, she also turned.

Maybe she *was* blacked out. Or maybe she had brain damage from lack of oxygen for too long. Because what she saw made no sense.

Howard Randall was standing in the shadows. He was holding Avery's Glock, pointing it at Biel.

"What are *you* doing here?" Biel asked.

Howard answered with two shots. Both caused Biel to stumble backward. After the second, he dropped to a knee. As Avery scrambled away from the edge of the platform, she saw that both shots had been to the gut.

Howard approached, the gun still leveled at Biel. He looked at Biel curiously, and then at Avery. He then looked back behind them. The sound of sirens approaching was growing louder. Through the haze of her mind, Avery thought they might be two blocks away now.

"You call it, Detective," Howard said. "Does he die or do we see if he can make it to the hospital once your friends get here? And then, I'm assuming, a very long prison sentence."

Kill him.

It was on her tongue and the fact that it would be someone else delivering the death freed her of any moral dilemma. But as she started to regain her breath, the events of the last few days caught up to her and she felt herself losing control. She was shuddering, shaking—not crying yet but feeling a torrent of sorrow coming forward.

She knew her duty. She was not supposed to kill if the subject could be brought in. Four gunshots, a hell of a beating, and an ankle

153

that might not ever be useful again. She'd done her best and now had the chance to deliver Biel.

"Prison," she said. "Let him rot."

Howard nodded and then looked to the Glock. "You hear that, Biel?" he asked.

Biel had nearly fallen over now but Howard held him steady, placing a hand on his shoulder.

"She's a good detective," Howard said. "And she has a good heart. She says you're going to prison. I, however, think that's too good for you. And since my moral compass deteriorated long ago…"

He placed the gun underneath Biel's jaw and pulled the trigger. Avery jumped at the sound of the shot. Blood splattered against Howard's face but he barely seemed to notice.

As Biel's body hit the concrete, Howard walked over to Avery. She cringed away from him and he smiled.

"I wouldn't hurt you," he said.

He looked to have more to say but the roar of sirens was too close now. Headlights broke the night as at least three cars came down toward the old platform.

Howard smiled.

"We had a good run, huh?"

She wondered what he was doing to do, and had a sudden surge of panic.

"Howard…just drop the gun. Go peacefully."

He smirked at her.

"I think we're beyond that now, Detective Black. We've always been beyond that."

The first car appeared, blinding them with their headlights. Then the second and the third. Car doors opened and people started shouting. She was pretty sure she heard O'Malley in there somewhere.

"Howard Randall, drop that gun and hit your knees. If you fail to do so, we *will* take you down."

Howard lifted the gun, pointing at the cars.

Two shots were fired his way. One of them caused Howard to stumble backward.

Avery was horrified as Howard fell, nearly doing a back flip into the water.

The moment he splashed in, every cop on the scene came rushing forward. There was a flurry of voices and movement that, in the play of headlights and shadows, was far too chaotic for Avery to follow.

"Avery…shit…Avery, are you okay?"

It was O'Malley. She nodded and when he took her hand, she squeezed it. "Rose," she said. "She okay?"

"Still sleeping," he answered. "We have five guys at the motel. Connelly and Finley are leading them."

She nodded again.

"Avery?"

She tried to respond but she couldn't. This time when the dark veil tried to drop down over everything, she let it. Because now, it did not feel like giving up. Now, it simply felt like rest…and that was something she thought she deserved.

She gave in to it as the flurry of activity carried on all around her. One of the last things she heard before the dark tide pulled her under was a very alarmed cop, screaming that they didn't have eyes on him.

Howard Randall was nowhere to be seen.

CHAPTER THIRTY THREE

The worst part of her recovery in the weeks that followed was that she missed Ramirez's funeral. The battle with Biel had done significant damage, the worst being an infection caused by being pierced by the old piece of pallet wood. She'd run a fever of one hundred and four for a day and a half and was far too weak to attend the services.

She'd also received a fractured jaw and a concussion. When she had come to roughly ten hours after she'd passed out underneath Newman's Wharf, she'd found her jaw swollen and wired shut. Rose had been there, sitting at her bedside. She'd done her best to walk her mother through what the doctors had reported: an infection, fractured jaw, a concussion, two broken ribs, a sprained wrist.

Rose had been the first to tell her that she would not be able to make it to Ramirez's funeral. Rose had stepped up and gone in her place. She'd told Avery about the service as well as she could but she'd spent most of the effort in tears.

For three days, Avery went in and out of consciousness. Sometimes there was someone there in the room with her. It was usually Rose, but Finley and O'Malley had also made appearances.

On her fourth day, she came to and was able to follow what her doctor was saying. He was a tall man, a little older but fetchingly handsome. He sat carefully on the edge of her bed and gave her the best bedside grin he could.

"You've been through hell," the doctor said. "And your daughter tells me you were upset about not being able to make it the funeral of your friend. I hope you understand that as your doctor, I had to make that call."

She only nodded. She cried several times while her jaws were wired shut and it had not been comfortable. It had actually been a little humiliating. Even worse was that she could only drink through a straw and she'd had to have Rose hold the cup for her the first few times.

"Hopefully you'll forgive me for that over time," the doctor went on. "Also, hopefully this good news will help. Tests this morning show that the infection is completely gone. Also, as long as X-rays check out today, we can probably un-wire your jaw tomorrow. The fracture wasn't that bad, but it was in a tricky place. We had to be absolutely cautious and take no chances. The ribs will take some time to heal and we're going to want to keep an eye on your head due to the concussion. Your wrist should be okay within a week or so. And I think that about covers it."

He then handed her a pad and a pen from the breast pocket of his doctor's jacket. "Do you have any other questions for me?" he asked.

She thought about it for a moment and then scribbled down: *Howard Randall?*

The doctor frowned and shrugged. "I've not heard much about the aftermath of your brawl," he said. "If you're up to it, I think I can allow one of the men that have been in and out for the last few days to come by and speak with you. Any preference?"

Again, she wrote down a name: *O'Malley.*

"I'll see how quickly I can get him here," the doctor said. "Also, you should know that your daughter has not left your side. She did make it to the funeral but other than that, she's been a resident of the hospital these last four days. So…anything else?"

Avery shook her head. The doctor took his leave and left her to the quiet room. A few minutes later, Rose came into the room. She had a container from the cafeteria. She smiled at her mother, seeing that she seemed to be wholly coherent for the first time in days.

She came over and kissed Avery on the forehead. "How ya doing, Mom?" she asked.

Avery used the pad the doctor had left and wrote down *Been better. Living, tho.* She paused for a moment and then started writing again. This took a bit longer and when she was done, she showed her note to Rose.

I love you and I love that you have stayed here. But things are safe now. Go home. Get some sleep. Get a shower. Eat a good meal. Don't waste away here. I know what that's like and it sucks.

Rose shook her head. "I've thought about it, but I can't. After everything that happened, I'm too scared. I'm not proud to admit it, but it's the truth."

Avery nodded her understanding and patted the side of the bed. She scooted over, grimacing through the pain in her ribs and wrist.

Rose didn't even bother to pretend that she wasn't going to take the invitation. She carefully crawled into bed beside her mother. Avery couldn't hold her like she wanted to, so she simple closed her eyes against the simple presence of her daughter. And with that sense of security, she fell into the first natural sleep she'd had for the last five days.

157

***

The X-rays had come back with stellar results and Avery was able to have the wires removed from her jaw the following day. The result was having the entire lower half of her face feel sore, almost like her jaw had been stretched into taffy. She was given a list of foods she could eat for the next two weeks (it wasn't very long) and asked not to speak at great length unless it was absolutely necessary.

Due to this, the conversation she had with O'Malley that afternoon was fairly quick and to the point. When he came into the room, Rose was there, sitting in the visitor's chair and scrolling through Facebook. Her friends were sending get well wishes to her mother, as well as letting her know how much of a bad-ass her mother was. News of what had happened was all over local news programs and Avery had become something of a hero.

When O'Malley entered, Rose waved a hello and got up from the chair. As she headed for the door to give them some privacy, Avery stopped her.

"No. Stay."

It hurt her jaw to say something so simple but it was a slight pain in comparison to what she had endured five nights ago.

"She's right," O'Malley said. "Sit back down, Rose. You went through hell, too. You're part of this, so you deserve updates, too."

Rose bit back a smile as she returned to her seat. She set her phone down and gave O'Malley he undivided attention.

"First," O'Malley said, "Connelly is getting pretty damn tired of answering calls from the media, requesting interviews with you. We're talking CNN and Fox News. The story about your fight with Biel went viral on Twitter. You're a meme now. It's getting out of hand."

She shook her head. The idea that what she had gone through was now of national interest was a little creepy to her. But she knew how news tended to spread…especially news involving a serial killer.

"A few things before we get to the information I know you're looking for. There are going to be small monuments created for Ramirez, Sawyer, and Dennison. We don't know where they'll go up yet, but we aren't making any solid plans until you're cleared to leave here. We want you involved in that. Cool?"

"Cool."

158

"Okay. Now…Howard Randall. We know he was shot at least once. Four officers saw it and can confirm. Some of his blood was also found on the scene. But the question we've been dying to know is this: Why was he there? Was he working *with* Biel?"

Avery shook her head. "He saved me."

"What?"

She reached for the pad and pen on the desk by the bed, but O'Malley waved her hands away. "No. Tell me later, when you can go into detail. Anyway…it's been five days, and we still can't find him. If the shot killed him and he sank to the bottom, we'll eventually find him with a scuba team. But you know how that works…if he was shot and killed and fell in, his body would have floated. But it didn't. And we have no idea where he is."

Avery nodded, but she was still hung up on what she had just told O'Malley. Speaking it out loud had solidified it—now she just had to figure out what it meant.

He saved me.

"We do have confirmation that inmates saw the two of them talking on at least two occasions while in prison. One of those conversations seemed to have gotten heated. And really, that's all the information we have."

She smiled and gave a weak nod.

And with Howard, she thought, *that's probably all you're going to get.*

CHAPTER THIRTY FOUR

Within another month, the pains from that night were still prominent. Everything had healed as well as it could, but the stitching in her calf itched all the time and her ribs still ached almost casually even though they were healing as well as the doctors could hope.

Still, she was able to live a somewhat normal life. She had been discharged from the hospital the day after her conversation with O'Malley. She and Rose had moved back into her apartment, grateful to find that a few guys in the A1 had paid to have her window replaced and the apartment cleaned.

The memorial ceremony for Ramirez, Sawyer, and Dennison came and went. It was a touching ceremony and the first time Avery had shown her face since the night by the wharf. Rose had shown her a few posts from Facebook where people were appreciative of what she had done and the way she had fought. Still, Avery felt she deserved none of it. She had declined all offers for interviews and after two weeks of it, people stopped calling. The world moved on to other stories and Avery was glad to have been left behind.

Through it all, as her wounds healed and her relationship with Rose continued to become something she could have only dreamed of in the past, she knew that in order to truly move on there were two things she needed to do. She wasn't looking forward to either of them, but they were necessary.

The first of those things occurred after the ceremony. She had gone into the A1 for the first time since coming home from the hospital. Everyone looked at her as if she were a celebrity or some sort of legend—which made what she was about to do so much easier.

She'd walked into Connelly's office slowly. She placed her gun and her badge on the corner of his desk. He only sighed at her and gave her a smile—a rarity for Connelly. He looked like he wanted to argue with her but shut it down before he could start.

"You sure about this?" he asked.

She nodded. She was afraid that if she tried to speak, she'd start crying. And she'd done more than enough of that over the last two or three weeks.

"I figured you would," he said. "But listen to me: if you change your mind, there's no question on my end. You come back in, pick these up, and you're back with the A1. I don't care if you're sixty and just going to ride a desk and answer calls. You're always welcome back here."

"Thanks," she said, leaving as quickly as she could without being rude.

When she was back in her car and allowed herself to openly weep, she headed directly from the A1 headquarters to the second place she needed to go to put it all behind her. It was a place she knew she had to visit—a location that would end this harrowing chapter of her life.

***

Ramirez's grave was simple yet elegant in a refined way. It had also been adorned with several flowers and bouquets from friends, family, and members of the Boston Police Department. When Avery approached it, she did so with a respect and sadness that she had known would level her—but not quite this badly.

Seeing his name engraved on the stone drove it home. He was gone and he was not coming back. She'd done her part to bring the man who had killed him to justice and for now, she could live with that. The inclusion of Howard Randall in that equation still confounded her, but not enough to distract her from why she was here.

She took a seat in front of the grave, sitting with her left leg extended as not to overexert the wound in her calf.

"I wish I could at least know if you were awake when he got there. Did you see him when he came in? Did you fight right away? Or were you sleeping?" She paused here and pounded the ground with her fist. "I'm so sorry…"

The hell of it was that now, a month removed from it all, she knew that there was no real reason to blame herself. There was no way she could have predicted Biel's path of destruction—or the level of his madness. But for the first two weeks or so, there had been plenty of blame and guilt rattling around in her head. Without Rose at her side to talk it out of her, there was no telling what state she might currently be in.

She fell silent again, partly because she wasn't sure what else to say, and partly because her jaw was starting to ache. Avery wasn't sure if she believed in God, an afterlife, or anything like that—which, considering that she was over forty might be something she needed to iron out later on down the road. Still, despite her uncertainty of those things, she was surprised at how comforting it was to speak to Ramirez as if there was no doubt that he could hear her from some other place.

"By the way, I handed in my gun and badge today. I have no idea what I'll do with the rest of my life. Rose seems to think I could make a living writing books about my cases, or looking into some sort of reality show nonsense. It's ridiculous how much attention I got over this. You would have gotten a kick out of it..."

That's when she started crying again. But it was a good sort of crying, a refreshing act that felt right while sitting at Ramirez's final resting place.

"I have the ring," she said. "When you were first admitted, a nurse found it on you and gave it to me. It may seem like poor judgment on her part, but we weren't sure you were going to make it."

She smiled and wiped away tears.

"I wish I'd had a chance to see your face when you gave it to me," she said. "I wish I'd had a chance to hear how you would propose." She cried freely now. "I'm sure it would've been in some wise-ass way," she added, and laughed through her tears.

She cried for a long time, until finally she calmed.

She stood, and stared down at his grave for a long time.

"And I wish you'd had a chance to hear my answer," she finally said, her voice soft now. "My answer is Yes. For now and forever—yes."

CHAPTER THIRTY FIVE

Three months later, Rose told Avery that she found an apartment she liked. They were still living together, Rose having still been traumatized by everything that had happened. But she was getting better about it all. The fact that Rose had found a place was a big step, and Avery was excited to see it with her tonight.

As Avery straightened up the apartment while Rose was out, she started to really look forward to the night. She ran a few errands that afternoon, picking up some things for dinner and running a fresh batch of flowers to Ramirez's grave.

When she returned to her apartment building, she checked her mailbox on the first floor and headed upstairs. As she ascended the stairs, she rifled through the handful of mail she'd gotten: a flier for a sale, her utility bill, junk mail from a credit card company, and a postcard.

The postcard made no sense. It was from Omaha, Nebraska. It had no message on the back and had been postmarked three days ago.

Who do I know in Nebraska?

The answer was easy: no one.

Then the real answer came to her. And although there was no reason to believe she was right, every nerve in her body knew it was so.

The postcard was from Howard. A postcard with no message from a random place in the country. It wasn't quite a riddle, but it practically screamed Howard.

She finally made it to her apartment, still eyeing the postcard. She had thought about him a lot lately. She was well aware that she'd likely be dead if Howard had not showed up that night. As to the *why*...well, she had theories but nothing certain. He had saved her, that was obvious, but had that been his plan all along?

She knew that there was an active ongoing search for him. His name was on the FBI's Most Wanted list, but it was buried on it, somewhere in the high teens. She knew they'd never catch him.

And a small part of her was glad.

A TRACE OF DEATH
(A Keri Locke Mystery--Book #1)

"A dynamic story line that grips from the first chapter and doesn't let go."
--Midwest Book Review, Diane Donovan (regarding Once Gone)

From #1 bestselling mystery author Blake Pierce comes a new masterpiece of psychological suspense.

Keri Locke, Missing Persons Detective in the Homicide division of the LAPD, remains haunted by the abduction of her own daughter, years before, never found. Still obsessed with finding her, Keri buries her grief the only way she knows how: by throwing herself into the cases of missing persons in Los Angeles.

A routine phone call from a worried mother of a high-schooler, only two hours missing, should be ignored. Yet something about the mother's voice strikes a chord, and Keri decides to investigate.

What she finds shocks her. The missing daughter—of a prominent senator—was hiding secrets no one knew. When all evidence points to a runaway, Keri is ordered off the case. And yet, despite pressure from her superiors, from the media, despite all trails going cold, the brilliant and obsessed Keri refuses to let it go. She knows she has but 48 hours if she has any chance of bringing this girl back alive.

A dark psychological thriller with heart-pounding suspense, A TRACE OF DEATH marks the debut of a riveting new series—and a beloved new character—that will leave you turning pages late into the night.

"A masterpiece of thriller and mystery! The author did a magnificent job developing characters with a psychological side that is so well described that we feel inside their minds, follow their fears and cheer for their success. The plot is very intelligent and

will keep you entertained throughout the book. Full of twists, this book will keep you awake until the turn of the last page."
--Books and Movie Reviews, Roberto Mattos (re Once Gone)

Book #2 in the Keri Locke series is also now available!

Blake Pierce

Blake Pierce is author of the bestselling RILEY PAGE mystery series, which includes ten books (and counting). Blake Pierce is also the author of the MACKENZIE WHITE mystery series, comprising six books (and counting); of the AVERY BLACK mystery series, comprising five books; and of the new KERI LOCKE mystery series, comprising four books (and counting).

An avid reader and lifelong fan of the mystery and thriller genres, Blake loves to hear from you, so please feel free to visit www.blakepierceauthor.com to learn more and stay in touch.

BOOKS BY BLAKE PIERCE

RILEY PAIGE MYSTERY SERIES
ONCE GONE (Book #1)
ONCE TAKEN (Book #2)
ONCE CRAVED (Book #3)
ONCE LURED (Book #4)
ONCE HUNTED (Book #5)
ONCE PINED (Book #6)
ONCE FORSAKEN (Book #7)
ONCE COLD (Book #8)
ONCE STALKED (Book #9)
ONCE LOST (Book #10)

MACKENZIE WHITE MYSTERY SERIES
BEFORE HE KILLS (Book #1)
BEFORE HE SEES (Book #2)
BEFORE HE COVETS (Book #3)
BEFORE HE TAKES (Book #4)
BEFORE HE NEEDS (Book #5)
BEFORE HE FEELS (Book #6)

AVERY BLACK MYSTERY SERIES
CAUSE TO KILL (Book #1)
CAUSE TO RUN (Book #2)
CAUSE TO HIDE (Book #3)
CAUSE TO FEAR (Book #4)
CAUSE TO SAVE (Book #5)

KERI LOCKE MYSTERY SERIES
A TRACE OF DEATH (Book #1)
A TRACE OF MUDER (Book #2)
A TRACE OF VICE (Book #3)
A TRACE OF CRIME (Book #4)

CPSIA information can be obtained
at www.ICGtesting.com
Printed in the USA
LVHW02s2149010818
585625LV00023B/253/P